STALKING JUSTICE

FRACTURED MINDS SERIES BOOK 1

KATE ALLENTON

COASTAL ESCAPE PUBLISHING, LLC

Published by Coastal Escape Publishing

Discover other titles by Kate Allenton
At

http://www.kateallenton.com

1

Today, I'd experienced death for the hundredth time. Like a sick anniversary that I'd never celebrate. The cool leather against my back and the sound of the heart monitor beeping in the room were the only two things that kept me grounded in this twisted game of hide and seek. I closed my eyes and inhaled. Anger and rage skirted my spine, crawling through my body like a killer virus in the veins.

I exhaled and found my target.

The killer's rage thrummed erratically. He was already in a kill zone. I seized hold of the feeling and closed my eyes, embracing the killer's energy as if it were a repeat of the first crime scene. My heart rate raced, syncing with his energy and subconsciously merging and melding with my own feelings.

He'd started without me.

I grabbed on to the tendril trails of his energy and the anger surrounding it and reeled myself to his location, like a fisherman trying to bring in his catch. This killer was unlike the other's I'd stalked; he evaded me the last two times I tried to ID him during the crimes. Death cloaked his identity like dirty windows, keeping me from getting enough of a description to fully inform the others. His rage during the kill was the only way I could track him. And tonight, was the night. I'd felt it stirring in my belly since my morning cup of coffee. It gathered like a perfect storm ready to break free every Friday without fail for the last three weeks. He'd killed, and I'd born witness just like the one he had tied to the bed now.

The acrid taste of metal covered my mouth as I inhaled the coppery scent of blood. The knife left a crimson line from the blade as he slowly dragged it across the victim's pale chest. Blood oozed from the deep gash and only worsened as she struggled against the ropes binding her wrists and ankles. The bed creaked beneath the killer's knees as he cleaned the blade by running it over the woman's pale cheek, marking her with her own blood.

This creep was a sick bastard, but then most serial killers were. Like an audio version of a horror flick, I repeated every horrific minute detail down to the terror in the woman's eyes.

"Blonde hair, green eyes." I squeezed my eyes tighter when all I wanted to do was open them and break the vision and make it go away. "Petite. It looks like she's in her own home. She's lying on a pink flowered comforter. He's already stripped her, and she has shallow cuts all over her body."

"You've got to give me more, Red. A time, a location, anything." Grant Mathew's urgent tone filled my ears. A voice I knew all too well as he repeated the same tired words he said the last hundred times we stalked killers using nothing more than my ability to tap into energy from the first crime scene.

There were a dozen people in this secret division just like me. Some people called us watchers, but I preferred the term hunters. Grant Mathews was an enforcer, my handler, and my brother-in-law. He was the guy who set the traps and took these psychopaths out of play. The worst were killed like feral animals, making the world a better place.

"Let me see if I can link into her point of view. Maybe I'll see something else." I hated this part. Seeing the victim and crimes through the killer's eyes were one thing, but seeing the cold dead eyes of the killer always rattled me to the core.

"You're safe, Lucy." Grant's words were meant to be soothing and put me at ease. There was nothing about my job that could accomplish that task. "Lock on the target and give me a damn face." The tension in Grant's gruff voice vibrated through the room, making my job harder.

"Shut up and let me concentrate." I took several deep breaths and moved my energy into the woman's, settling in as if it were my second skin. The bold move was the only way I'd be able to stop this crime from actually taking place. I inhaled a sharp breath as pain radiated across my chest. My lungs struggled to expand as I tried to break away from the woman's tangled web of emotions. The fear clogging her entire body was a gift and a curse. I needed her terror to connect, but it kept me rooted as if stuck in a spider web trying to break free. Remembering I wasn't the poor soul in danger calmed me, but only a little.

"He's wearing a creepy black ski mask," I whispered, trying to catch my breath.

"What color are his eyes?"

"Unnaturally bright blue, almost neon looking."

"Contacts. Any visible identifying markings?"

I slowly let my gaze run over him and braced myself as he lifted the knife to his shoulder. I spotted a telling sign and smiled. "He has a tat on his wrist. A box with lines. It looks like a barcode."

"Is it day or night? Can you see the window or a clock?"

"I can't tell. She's not looking. I'll have to break the connection with her and just view."

"Stay with her," Grant ordered. "Give me more about him before you view the room."

The killer froze with the knife in the air and slowly lowered it, making my blood curdle. "I knew you'd come, Lucy," he whispered to the blonde. The panic racing through the woman's body escalated, a feeling echoed in my own body, connected as we were. Confusion clouded her. "That's why I'm taking my time with this one. She's special, just like you and your sister."

"Oh shit." The heart monitor machine beeped frantically in the silent room. "He knows I'm watching, and he knows my name and about Gigi."

I gripped the side of the bed I was lying on as blood rushed through my ears.

"Give me more, Lucy," Grant whispered, resting a warm hand over mine.

The killer lifted the knife again and narrowed his eyes. "This kill is on your head. She's going to die because of you." He grinned. "Your sister will too. Have you missed her today?"

He ran the knife over the victim's neck, and I stretched mine in response and turned my head. I knew what was coming next. Every painful second. The poor woman was going to die, and it wasn't going to be quick.

"Allison Tanner first and then Gigi next. She's waiting at home, so anxious for you to save her," the killer whispered seconds before the sharp blade slowly cut the victim's throat.

I gurgled, as did the victim, too startled by the murderer's words to shield myself from the slicing pain. Grant squeezed my hand as if trying to absorb what I was going through.

"Allison Turner, and he claims Gigi is next," I said, finding my voice, struggling to stay in the moment. I moved my energy out of the woman's and viewed the scene as a bystander. My gaze went to the window. "It's daytime," I said and moved toward the window in search of her location. Blue doors lined the building across the street. The familiar sound of my neighbors' kids playing baseball on the street below. My eyes shot open as fear raged through my body, making it difficult to breathe. "It's my building. Third floor."

That hadn't been all I'd reported seeing. I'd seen much more after the group ran out the door hunting the killer. I, on the other hand, wasn't quick to move. I continued lying on the bed and closed my eyes again, connecting like I had before, only this time with sheer determination and will as my guide.

I stayed connected with him and watched as he drove through the suburban neighborhood, parked his sedan in the drive, and entered his suburban home at 2134 Wyoming Road. I watched him as he showered away the death he'd inflicted before changing into his mailman delivery uniform and peeked down into the cellar. Every nerve in my body tightened as he confirmed my worst nightmare. My sister was tied up in a chair, her head lolled to the side, and her shirt ripped and dirty. Anger, either his or mine, stirred in my gut. When I was connected, it was hard to tell whose emotions I was channeling. I slowly opened my eyes.

"Time's up, asshole."

Gone was the despair that I'd felt prior. The killer had escaped capture, but he'd never escape me. I slowly sat up and tossed my feet over the edge of the bed. Grabbing my backpack by the door, I slid it up my arm. I'd made a silent promise that today would be the killer's last deadly deed, and I had every intention of keeping it.

Breaking into his house had been a simple tumble of the locks. I cleared the house and yanked the phone from the wall before easing down into the basement.

"I'm here," I whispered to Gigi. "I'm getting you out of here."

I used one of the bloodstained knives sitting on a nearby table and cut Gigi's bindings. She slumped forward into my arms.

"He's going to come back." Gigi said as her head lolled to the side.

Wrapping my arm around her waist, I eased her up from her spot and helped her out to my car. It wasn't until the next day, when she was safe and in the hospital that I went back to follow through on my promise.

I took my time to venture around his house. I was almost certain that he'd skip town knowing Gigi was free. Whether it was arrogance or stupidity, I'd been wrong.

I'd found his stash of mementos and his weapon of choice. I studied each of them and laid them out on the breakfast table. There were three more victims the government didn't even know existed. An hour later I sat in his darkened house with nothing more than my breath and racing heartbeat to keep me company. My tools lay in the bag at my feet, and I held the cool grip of the gun in my hand. The sound of an engine and the flash of headlights through the window were my only indications that my fun was about to begin. The door opened and closed before he flicked on the lights. He turned and froze in place as he peered down the barrel of my silencer.

"Hello, Carl." I pulled the trigger, taking his ability to flee.

2

Doctor Marsh held the file to his chest as the live feed from the psych ward surveillance played on the screen. "They found her blood at the crime scene."

"If she's a killer, why is she here instead of sitting on death row?"

"You'd have to ask those questions to someone with higher clearance than mine, although I'd guess the jury took into account the extenuating circumstances. The man she stalked had kidnapped her sister."

"She doesn't look dangerous. She looks like one strong gust would blow her over."

The video on the screen showed a woman wearing the standard-issue psych ward uniform. Her blonde hair was tucked neatly behind her ears as she stood in line to get her meds. Her gaze wasn't on the floor like most of the patients. It was across the room on another woman standing near the window. Her eyes narrowed to slits. They moved at the same time as if in sync.

"Who's that?" Special Agent Noah Roth asked.

"Margo." The doctor sighed.

Margo was tall and didn't look like she missed any meals. If there were a woman's football team, she could easily play a linebacker. The scowl on her face and clenched fists might mean trouble. Margo crossed the room to an old lady sitting at a table eating a pudding cup. She snatched the pudding cup from the old lady's hands and began to eat the chocolate with her fingers.

She got in one fingerful before Lucy reached her and shoved Margo away. Margo tossed the dessert onto the ground and was the first to swing.

She missed. Lucy's didn't.

It wasn't until the guards broke things up that Noah realized Lucy Bray wasn't a victim. She was the threat.

Lucy was given her meds and a paper cup of water and downed them. Grabbing the supplied pudding cup, she gave it to the old lady who was now missing hers. Margo was across the room having a nurse attend to her busted lip.

"Does Lucy always fight over pudding?" Agent Roth asked.

"Lucy doesn't like bullies, and Margo thinks she runs the place. She tries to take Francine's pudding every day. We've had multiple issues with Margo and Lucy stopping her. Don't be fooled by Lucy's stature, Agent Roth. She singlehandedly accomplished what law enforcement couldn't."

"She figured out who the perp was that kidnapped her sister."

The doc handed Noah her file. "She tracked him, tortured him, and then left him in a coma just like her sister. She saved her twin sister's life but by time Lucy got her to the hospital, Gigi had already slipped into a coma too. I think that's why Lucy left him the way she did. She blamed herself for not getting there sooner."

"Are you sure she didn't have help?" he asked. "She doesn't look like the killer type. Fighter sure, but not a killer."

The doctor smiled like he'd been impressed by her deeds. "She dragged his unconscious body into the police station, dropped the souvenir pictures she'd found of the killer's other victims over his body, dropped to her knees, and laced her fingers behind her head. There was no question she did the deed."

Roth flipped open Lucy's file and skimmed her report before turning to the picture of the shirtless unconscious man in the lobby of the police department. The perp had several wounds, but none were as prominent as his lacerated throat and each slice over his chest.

"I'm surprised he didn't die. Lucky for him, it looks like she missed every major artery."

"She didn't miss. It was strategic. She gave him the same injuries he gave his victims. She is medically trained. She was a straight A med student moonlighting as a participant in some super-secret governmental program until this happened. Hell, she has a doctorate in psychology," Doctor Marsh explained. "They never found Carl Chisolm's missing finger."

Marsh turned his gaze to the screen again. Lucy Bray was now talking with two other women, who looked ready to fight again.

Roth gave a slow nod. "Has she had any other incidents since arriving besides the bully?"

"Lucy sticks up for the weaker patients in the group. She's a loner, but she's lethal when provoked. She may be brave when awake, but Lucy has nightmares she hasn't been able to shake."

"Does she talk about them? Ever tell you what they are about?"

"She claims the man she put in a coma torments her dreams. Crazy, right?"

Agent Roth remained silent.

"Forgive me for saying, but you don't appear to know much about Lucy. Why do you need to see her?"

"That's classified." Roth snapped the file closed. "Bring her to me."

Lucy was handcuffed before being led out of the common room. It was standard practice when dealing with the mental ward inmates, especially the ones with attempted murder attached to their names. The doctor escorted her to the conference room and opened the door.

"Lucy, this is Special Agent Roth."

Her gaze traveled slowly around the room before finally settling on him as he sipped water from his cup.

"Release her restraints." Roth gestured to the handcuffs around her wrist.

"No, it's better this way," Lucy said and moved to a

chair, pulling it out. She sat, placing her hands in her lap beneath the table.

"Why did you keep the restraints?" Roth asked, leaning back in the chair.

"For your protection. I might not like what you're here to say," she answered.

"I'm FBI Special Agent Noah Roth."

She glanced at the file sitting between them. "Why are you here?"

"Straight to the point, I like that." Roth flipped open the file. "Why did you torture Carl Chisolm?"

"He's a sick sadistic serial killer, and someone had to do the job. It's in my file if you would have taken the time to read it." Lucy's face remained unchanged, not even the slightest hint of remorse in her voice.

"What makes you think I haven't read your file and know everything there is to know about you?"

This time she smiled sweetly. "The pen in your pocket."

He patted his pocket. "What about my pen?"

"It's the perfect weapon for jabbing into your artery. You'd bleed out before the locks on the door could even be disengaged." She turned her gaze to the window. "The window in this room has no bars, which is an error of judgment, either on your part or the staff's for not insisting on a more secure location to meet. You must not believe I'm a threat." She raised a brow and continued. "I was cross country running champ in high school. They won't be able to catch me if I wanted to escape."

"Assuming you could get over the iron fence," he added.

"Are you a hundred percent sure that I can't?" she asked.

She turned her gaze to the empty holster. He'd checked that particular gun in when he'd arrived. The one strapped at his ankle was another story. She glanced under the table and grinned. "And that gun at your ankle. You should think twice about wearing one to meet with an attempted murderer. Not that I'd need it. I'd go for the pen." She leaned in and lowered her voice. "Quieter and less fuss, although a bit messier."

"That would be kind of hard to do in handcuffs."

Her smile slowly disappeared as she tossed the handcuffs onto the table between them. "If you'd read my file, you would have known I can escape these restraints."

"Magician and murderer," he said.

"I've got nothing but time on my hands. As you can imagine, they don't give me many toys, and I've read all the books in the library." She let out a healthy sigh and clasped her hands together, resting them on the table. "So why don't you cut the crap, Special Agent Roth, and tell me what you want?"

Roth flipped the file closed. "I want to know how it's possible you can track a killer when the police can't."

"It's classified, but I'm guessing you already know that answer."

"You're skilled." He held her gaze.

"My level of expertise varies."

"Judging by your IQ, I'd say you're more than just a tracker. Some might even call you a stalker, possibly a hunter."

She shrugged and leaned back in her chair. "You wouldn't be wrong to think that. Actually, that might make you smarter than the rest."

"Can you do it again?"

Lucy lifted her brow and tilted her head. "Now why would I do that? So you can keep me in here longer?"

Roth slipped the five pictures of the dead college-aged girls out of his pocket and spread them out in front of Lucy. "Someone is killing more women."

Lucy sighed. "I'm already doing time for a crime because the government failed to take care of their mess. Did you know in addition to Carl's postal job, he worked part time as security for the division where I'd started as a participant and then employed? It's why he wore a mask. He knew I could identify him. Granted, it was a false sense of security."

"And you think that makes it a government mess?"

"He used his badge as a license to terrorize and kill. Why do you think those women let him into the houses to begin with?"

"We're not all like him," Roth said, eyeing her with interest.

"Even so, why would I want to get involved with *your* case?"

She let her gaze linger on the pictures.

"These women were someone else's sisters and

daughters. You saved your sister, Gigi. I thought you might see the common link."

Her lips twisted. "You did read my file, only it wasn't this one. It was sealed. I'm impressed. Get the charges against me dropped, and we'll talk," Lucy said, rising and heading for the locked door.

"You know they'll never go for that."

"They will if they think I'm your last resort." Lucy paused by the door and turned back around as she slid the stolen security card key out of her sleeve. "Tell me, Special Agent Roth. Those kills were on the beach, right?"

His brows dipped, and he turned the picture back around to face him. "How do you know that? There is no sand in these pictures, not even a location."

"For one thing, they're all sunburned, but that wasn't the giveaway."

"What was?"

"You'll figure it out." She slid the card key through the lock, pulled the door open, and walked out just as easily as she'd walked in, only this time without an escort.

4

Noah Roth strode through the halls of the FBI building toward Intact Operations. He'd fought hard for this assignment, impressing the paper-pushers who made the decisions. This was his shot. The one chance he'd get to finally have everything he wanted.

This field office was unlike the others. This special task force employed only essential personnel. This was a trial group that had something to prove, a hodgepodge of players from various agencies and other questionable places had assembled to take on cases that the other agencies couldn't solve. Their mission wasn't just about the killer they were hunting. This division had potential to be so much more. They were only missing one link, and Noah had found it, but getting the others to agree would be a hard sell.

As he shoved open the meeting room door, all conversation ceased, and eyes turned to him. The commander of their unit, Diesel Hunt, sat at the head of the table. His overbearing presence kept them focused, and he called the shots. His vote was the only one that counted. "How did it go?"

That was a loaded question. "Lucy Bray was everything I hoped for and more. She's the one we need." He slid the pen out of his pocket and tossed it to Grant Mathews, Lucy's last handler. "She ignored the gun and mentioned the pen just like you said she would."

"I'm not surprised. I trained her." Grant grunted.

Diesel Hunt crossed his arms over his chest. His knowledge and skill made him the perfect candidate to assume the role of boss. His intimate knowledge and connection to the covert military operation that Lucy had been working for gave him much needed insight.

"We can't trust her not to go off the rails again," Hunt said.

"Her experience is exactly why we need her." Noah tossed the file onto the table. "She's not only smart and has the ability needed for the hunt, but she's resourceful, cunning, and determined. She's the one we need."

Diesel's expression didn't soften at his unpredictable choice. Lucy was the last person they should be pulling into the team. Everything about her crime proved she deserved to be sitting behind bars. "Explore other options. The institute has other watchers you can work with."

Four faces stared back at Noah. They almost had everything they needed to be successful in all of their endeavors. Sam Zachman, the hacker, could track any ghost Diesel Hunt gave him and find an electronic trail with little info. Carson Tines the squad's weapons expert with the ability to not only build anything they'd ever need but to cloak it from prying eyes. Ford Rain a world-class thief with the ability to infiltrate any structure. And Grant Mathews, who would never admit it, had been the one who put Lucy's name as a bug in Noah's ear. He was the muscle behind their team.

Noah knew his place in the motley crew. He'd been brought in under similar circumstances. He'd started as a liaison helping the FBI catch and track uncatchable thieves, knowing exactly how they worked because Noah's youth was just as dirty before he found his way. They were all a bunch of misfit vigilantes who now carried badges, although they played by a different set of rules.

Their rules that got shit done. They all had their demons and reasons for joining the team. None more so than the boss, Hunt, who was still living his nightmare.

"I've worked with all of the Mind Watchers. Lucy isn't a watcher. She's a stalker." Grant Mathews shoved the picture of Lucy's sister to the center of the table. "None are as gifted as Lucy. She connects with the emotional energy of the killer's tendencies from a single visit of the crime scenes or even the bodies. We called it the mind web, and she's the only one that can connect without the use of instruments. That makes her mobile. The others are just visionaries and stationary, predicting bits and pieces of the killer's actions. Lucy lives them vicariously through the connection." Grant's jaw ticked as he continued. "Lucy is the only one that can see and feel in real time."

"He knows her best." Noah pointed at Grant, Lucy's last handler in the program before she turned rogue.

"That doesn't make up for taking action into her own hands."

"She saved her twin sister, my wife. If she'd told me what she saw, I'd be the one behind bars, because he'd be six feet under instead of in a coma, like Gigi," Grant announced.

"She's unpredictable, and that's the last thing this team needs."

"She knew the women were killed at the beach just by the head pictures taken on the autopsy table."

Agent Hunt tilted back in his chair. His gaze was skeptical. "There were no indications in those pictures, and it hasn't made the news. How does she know?"

Noah shrugged and took a seat. "She wouldn't say. The point is that she knows things."

Even Grant seemed stunned that Lucy had known. "Has she had any visitors?"

"None on the books. I checked before talking to her doctor."

"Any new patients?" Hunt asked.

"I didn't ask." Noah's brows dipped. He hadn't considered that there might be an inside connection.

"I'm sure she'd do anything to get out of the ward," Diesel suggested.

"Quite the opposite, she was willing to stay and serve her time," Noah explained. "Her only demand was that if she helped catch the killer that she be released or nothing at all. There was no room to negotiate."

"There's always a way to get her to agree," Grant said, meeting Noah's gaze.

He was her family and her partner; he knew her best.

"Bring her in and let me talk to her while under observation," Grant said. "Offer her a little bit of freedom on a short leash and for God's sake, tell her the truth if she hasn't already figured it out. She's highly intelligent, so treat her like it." Grant scrubbed his face. "I agree with Noah. We need her."

5

LUCY

I'd counted the turns in my head even though they had placed me in the back of a prison vehicle with no windows.

Tha-thunk, tha-thunk. The Mason Bridge train tracks. I smiled. My home was only a twenty-minute hike to the east. Growing up in this town had its perks, even without the use of my eyes. This wasn't the first time I'd been blindfolded. The scent of sandalwood drifted in the confined space. A smell I knew well. The man didn't have to say a word. Grant Mathews was providing my escort.

The van slowed to a stop, and I stretched my back, pulling at my chains attached to the floor. "I guess they thought you could predict my every move and that I wouldn't kill you, Grant. Is that why they chose you?"

"They didn't chose me, Lucy." His voice washed over me like a familiar breeze. "I volunteered."

He slid the blindfold off my eyes. His smile was just as I remembered with a few more lines around his mouth from the last time he'd visited me with updates about Gigi. "How did you know it was me?"

The back doors opened, and the smell of the river drifted in. "You still wear the aftershave I gave you for Christmas three years ago, and you still do that unconscious sigh thing on car rides. Care to tell me what we're doing at the old mill?"

FBI Agent Noah Roth stood just outside the door. "I'm guessing she figured it out."

"Was there ever any doubt?" Grant said, releasing my cuffs. "The blindfold was useless. She even knows where we are."

I rubbed my wrists from the shackles. "The only thing I haven't figured out is what I'm doing here."

Grant rested his head against mine. "Don't run. I don't want to chase you."

"You wouldn't need to. Scrappy there has a Taser in one holster and a Beretta in the other. Seems like he took notes when I told him I was cross country champ."

"They know more than that about you, Lucy."

I patted his chest. "Thanks to you, I'm sure."

They led me out of the van, and I took a minute, lifting my face to the warmth of the sun. It was the little pleasures I missed most being in captivity. I stretched and let my gaze wander my surroundings, taking in everything in sight. The scent of nature and freedom in the air. Water lapping against the smooth stone barrier. The current was in full force. Freedom, if I cared to take it.

Two armed guards wearing military fatigues stood outside the door of the mill with rifles in hand. The windows didn't have any bars. The forest would give me cover if I didn't choose the river's current to whisk me away.

I let them guide me into the mill. If the outside was rustic and made of wood, the inside was a complete surprise; refurbished and modernized. On the outside, it looked like a standard mill, minus the men with guns; on the inside, it was so much more.

That manly smell competed with the solid oak beams, which had few splinters, running across the ceiling and attached to strategically sturdy posts from the floor to the ceiling. The sun shining through the bar-less windows lacked dust motes floating in the air.

The mill's interior was like the gooey center of a brownie without the sharp exterior edges that cut the soft pallet in a mouth. The motley crew of men inside were like pieces from different puzzles. They didn't look like they fit. The room smelled of gunpowder and masculinity. Both of which were combustible under the right triggers.

A man with spiky, dark purple hair sat in the center of the room we entered. On the walls were various large computer screens displaying surveillance of different places. The computer nerd glanced up at me. His bright smile was welcoming, if not a bit curious. His shirt told me enough. *Byte me.* He was a computer geek.

Another man was farther across the room, surrounded by a table of weapons and other deadly gear. He seemed lost in his own little world, yet looks could be deceiving. He might not have even glanced my way, but he knew I was in the room. His jaw tensed for a split second, giving him away.

The other man in the room wasn't a fed. His designer suit alone probably cost more than a run-of-the-mill agent's yearly salary. He kept his hands in his pockets as his gaze bored into mine.

Alone, each man could have been anyone. Together, well...that piqued my interest. I grinned as I was guided down a hall toward more rooms, only stopping at a typical interrogation room. Grant led me inside, and I stumbled into Noah before he had a chance to close the door. I smiled up at him apologetically. "Sorry. I'm such a klutz."

He patted the security badge attached to his suit and raised a brow. "Just checking." He met Grant's gaze and eased the door closed.

"What is this place?" I asked, walking to the mirror. I held my finger against it and noticed no gap. Interrogation-room style. I'd been in my share of similar rooms when I turned myself in.

"What do you think it is?" Grant asked, pulling out a chair facing the mirror for me to sit.

"No blood on the floor, no torture? It leaves the obvious with the chair, table, and the mirror," I answered, taking a seat. "The only question left is who the wizard is behind the curtain pulling the strings."

"Let me cut to the chase," Grant said.

"Gigi and I always adored that about you." I smiled, meeting his gaze for the first time since walking in.

"They aren't going to release you, but if things go right, they'll give you a short leash."

My eyes narrowed at the connotation. "I'm not an animal."

"You left Carl in a coma. To them, that makes you dangerous."

"Only to men with no souls. Does your puppeteer have one?" I sweetly smiled.

"Carl's starting to stir awake," Grant said.

"I know. I felt it," I answered. "Or have you forgotten that when I make a connection, only death can sever it? One of the many side effects from the experiment that *your* commander and scientist left out of the contract I had to sign."

"Does he still talk to you in your mind?"

"When my guard is down." I sat forward in my chair. The mental patient garb I was wearing felt itchy against my skin. "Now tell me why I'm here, or take me back. I'm missing my afternoon med cocktail, and I have to stop Margo from stealing everyone's dessert."

Grant opened the file, and I forgot to breathe. A thin gold necklace with a cross attached sat on top. A necklace identical to the ones our parents had given us on our sixteenth birthday before they died. Recognition smacked me in the face, as did my anger.

"Is that one mine or Gigi's?" I shoved to my feet, sending the chair flying back against the wall. Planting my hands on the table, I narrowed my gaze. "You better not have brought me here to tell me she's dead."

"You can rest assured I'm getting your sister the best treatment and doctors she needs."

I swallowed hard and stared at the necklace.

"I remember the day she got hers." Grant said as sadness filled his eyes.

My glare remained unmoved. Grant hadn't even hinted about this to me during his last visit. "You were high school sweethearts."

"She loved it even more than the engagement ring the day I proposed. Neither one of us could keep her safe, Lucy. Her abduction wasn't your fault. You have to believe that."

Emotions I'd compartmentalized rushed through me like a tsunami as I struggled not to go for his jugular and rip out his throat. "Make no mistake; we both failed her."

"No, Lucy." He shook his head. "We didn't fail her. You knew her best. She'd give the shirt off her back to a stranger. Carl used that against her, against us. If I'd have found him that day, he'd be six feet under instead of in the hospital, and I'd be the one sitting in jail. I need you to remember the anger, that feeling of fear of losing her, and tap into it to help us find another one." Grant lifted the gold chain. "Each dead girl had one of these around their necks and were inked with a tattoo that matches your and Gigi's birthmarks."

I shook my head and stood taller. Disbelief made it difficult to breathe. "That's impossible; Carl hasn't been released."

"No, he hasn't, Lucy. Carl wasn't working alone, either. He trained someone, and these calling cards were meant for you." Grant opened a file and pulled out crime scene photos, scattering them on the table.

They looked similar to the ones I'd seen, only the

faces of these girls looked identical to mine. "I don't understand."

"He uses silicone on their faces to get them to look identical to you and Gigi. We can only assume that he's killing them because they aren't convincing him that they're you. You're the ultimate prize he wants. Now help us catch this asshole so I can put a bullet through his head and we can finish this once and for all."

I slipped Noah's gun from the waistband of my clothes and slammed it on the table. "You won't need to if I do it first."

The door shoved open, and I met Noah's gaze. "What? Did you think you were the only one that could pull off stealing stuff? I figured out your identity. Noah Roth used to go by Noah Razinski. He took his mother's name when he was provided a new identity with the FBI as a liaison to catch criminals."

"How in the hell did you figure that out?"

"You left your fingerprints on the cup you were using. You saw how easy it was for me to move around. A few distractions and I pulled them. You guys have no clue what types of criminals are locked up in the psych ward. You thought I was bad before going into that place. It made me worse. Took less than twenty-four hours to have your real name, along with your rap sheet. It only cost me a pack of cigarettes, and I don't even smoke."

I glanced at the person still hiding behind the mirror. "Have you seen enough? I only have one condition, and it has nothing to do with my release."

Noah crossed the room and grabbed his gun. "I told you she was good."

Grant had a smile a foot wide on his face. "I warned them they had no idea."

I took a piece of paper and a pen and wrote down my demand. I slammed it up against the two-way mirror and raised my brow. I wasn't leaving the compound without them agreeing.

6

————

Twenty-four hours later, I stood on the hotel balcony of a penthouse suite in Panama City, Florida, listening to the sweet sound of waves crashing on the shore as a salty breeze caressed my face. I'd thought it would be years before I ever felt this again. I glanced down the ten floors of balconies, mentally calculating the best way to get down in the event of an emergency. I scanned the beach line. Five fishing boats were just offshore. There weren't really many places to run considering I didn't know how to swim.

I'd almost drowned once as a child during one of our yearly family vacations. Once had been enough. I had no plans to get my toes wet, but the idea of running in the packed sand spurred excitement, especially since it meant I could map the area. I turned to find Noah standing behind me with a bracelet dangling from his fingers.

"A present? You shouldn't have."

He stepped forward and clasped it around my wrist. "I

didn't." He grinned. "This is a tracker that was designed specifically for you. You're a smart girl; you know what a stun gun can do?"

"Yeah," I said, spinning the metal band around my wrist.

"Consider this a portable stun gun hooked up to a GPS feed." He pointed to the solid green light. "They've given you a ten-mile radius from the hotel, and you must be accompanied by one of us at all times. If you violate the area grid or try to escape, that light will flash ten times and a warning will sound before it goes to a solid red. Trust me when I tell you that you don't want that."

"What happens at red?"

"They'll hit you with volts of electricity in pulses that are guaranteed to slow you down. We have a satellite dedicated to watching your every move."

"This isn't a movie, Agent Roth. Something like that could kill me."

"It's not attached to the artery in your neck, Lucy." His lips twitched. "It's just a jolt that will disable you."

I tried to pull the bands apart, unsuccessfully. "Really, you shouldn't have."

Noah rested his hand over my fumbling fingers tugging at the bracelet. "I designed the locking mechanism. You won't get it off."

My lips twisted into a smile. "Challenge accepted. What happens if I'm kidnapped and taken out of your grid? Are you going to risk incapacitating me while in the hands of a killer?"

Noah grinned this time. "Yes, but don't worry; we won't be far behind to stop him."

Bait. The smile slipped from my lips. They'd use me as bait. No better than the fishermen on those damn boats offshore.

"I need to go for a run. Who's taking me?"

"There is no time for a run. We have a meeting with the locals and a few other agencies." Noah lifted his hands and stepped back, letting me walk into the suite.

The computer geek, Sam, had been talkative during the entire flight. He'd been unable to shut up, until now. He didn't even acknowledge the rest of us as he converted the main living quarters into the same setup he'd had at the mill. I couldn't stop myself from grinning as he tried to take the picture off the wall.

"It's probably bolted in place to keep the spring breakers from tearing it up."

"I spent all my spring breaks at space and math camps."

I'd just bet he did. I held out my hand. "I'm Lucy."

"I know who you are." He shrugged and went back to plugging up his equipment. "They warned me before the flight that you were as screwed up as an infected computer."

"I'm harmless," I answered and winked. "Harmless as a virus."

He rested his palm over his chest. "You speak puns."

I shrugged and laughed. "Doesn't everyone?"

He glanced at Noah. "Can we keep her?"

"She isn't a puppy, Sam. When she's finished with the assignment, she'll have to go back into the psych center."

"I'll have to visit," he said, going back to typing on the keyboard to boot the system up.

"I'm not allowed visitors," I interjected.

"If they have computers, I'll find a way."

"She's a killer, kid," Mr. Expensive Suit said from across the room. He was staring out at the ocean below. Grant had sat next to me on the private FBI plane, and he'd told me what he could of everyone on board, including fancy pants, his name but not much else about Ford Rain.

"Actually. I've never killed anyone," I said. "I could have, and probably should have, but I didn't," I said, grabbing my bag. I glanced back at Noah. "Where am I sleeping?"

"One of the bedrooms without windows," he said as he shoved open a door and gestured me inside.

It was a typical beach room. It could have been any one that my sister and I had vacationed in growing up. The seashell-printed bedspread and nautilus big rope décor covered the entire room. The queen-sized bed was bigger than I imagined. A small TV was hanging on the wall. I opened one of the two doors in the room to find a bathroom that was shared with another room. At that moment, the other side opened, and Ford Rain, fancy suit guy, was staring back at me.

"Looks like we're sharing."

"Looks like it," I said and shut the door. I checked out the closet before tossing my bag onto the bed to unpack.

I unzipped the bag and groaned at the clothes inside. They didn't pack me much, just a couple pairs of shorts and jeans and a few tops, along with some toiletries, which my brother-in-law had packed. My guess was he'd taken Gigi's things.

Whoever had been responsible sucked at the job. Nothing even remotely matched. I pulled each piece out, giving it a once-over before tossing it onto the bed. I settled for jeans and a concert T-shirt that had probably been given away to a thrift shop. I just prayed we didn't need to go anywhere important. If we did, I was sure to stand out like a neon sign on a dark night.

At least the toiletries were better.

Someone had packed my personal belongings from the psych ward, including my necklace, which had been confiscated. I slipped that over my head, feeling better already. I grabbed my toothbrush and toiletries and headed for the bathroom.

The door opened again, and Ford stood on the other side with a shaving bag in hand. "Looks like we may have to come up with a system."

"How about knocking?" I offered and stepped back into the room with the door handle in my grasp. "It's just a thought, assuming you don't want to see me naked."

His gaze slid down my body just as I shut the door. I plopped down on the bed after putting my clothes away. "From one cage to another."

7

Once we left the hotel, traffic on Front Beach Road crawled at a snail's pace. The route to the meeting at the Sherriff's Department was packed with shirtless guys hooting and hollering at half-clad women. A group of several girls lifted their fast food cups in the air when guys whistled as they passed by. What I wouldn't give to be that carefree, although I'd be more cautious about hiding my liquor.

I read through the pamphlets I'd taken off the check-in desk while waiting on the others earlier. The reading material reminded me of the things I wouldn't be doing on this trip. There were five of us packed like sardines in the SUV. The air conditioner was fighting a losing battle with the sultry confines of the car.

Carson, the weapons expert, who'd hardly looked at me the entire trip, had changed out if his black stretch military shirt that soaked up the sun's rays to an airy button-down flower printed shirt. Ford, the expensive suit guy, had ditched his jacket and rolled up his sleeves.

Grant, hadn't bothered to freshen up. Noah, sat behind the wheel. He'd only disappeared once while at the hotel when his phone had rung. The computer geek, Sam, had stayed behind at the hotel to finish playing with his toys.

It took us thirty minutes just to get down Front Beach Road through all of the partying college kids. I couldn't help but wonder which of the college-aged girls would be the killer's next victim. I swallowed hard, trying to forget that he was using me as his model to pick his victims.

The other side of the bridge was nothing like the beach side. Where people made reservations to play in the sun on the white sand, this was where the locals lived. This was real everyday life. We pulled up at the Sheriff's Department, got out of the car, and walked into the building.

The other three spoke in hushed tones. Grant stood near me while we waited. "You think we should add this to our vacation spots when you're out and Gigi wakes up?"

I shrugged. "Only if it's not spring break."

"I hear the offseason is for snowbirds."

"Assuming they let me out."

"Gentlemen, and..." The deputy lost his train of thought as he stared at me. "Uh...Ms. Bray, sorry the resemblance is uncanny."

"Dr. Lucy Bray," Noah corrected.

I might not have finished my med school training, but I'd gone in as a doctor in psychology.

"Pardon me, Dr. Bray. If you guys will follow me."

The Suit Guy we traveled with glanced over at me again, this time with curiosity in his eyes.

The door continued to buzz as we were led beyond the safety of the steel-enforced door into the inner office.

The place was built like a square with one hallway on each length. The smell was musty. Her nose twitched with an unreleased sneeze as if no one ever aired the place out. One side of the hall held offices, and the other was nothing but a long string of windows that looked into what appeared to be an atrium. "That's...unique."

"We call that the fishbowl," the deputy said as he continued to walk.

I could understand why. Watching the two uniformed officers conversing out in the greenery made me feel like a voyeur.

The deputy pushed open the double doors to reveal a conference room. Three men and one woman waited inside. Two men wearing uniforms, one dressed in a suit that probably cost twice as much as fancy pants in my party, and a petite blonde dressed like she was there to take notes. All talking stopped as they stared at me. I ignored their questioning looks and walked straight to the whiteboard, where pictures of the murder scene were being held in place by magnets. I swallowed hard at the resemblance. This killer was skilled. The prosthetics he used were almost spot-on. Almost.

Voices whispered behind me, but I tuned out the words. The victims didn't just look like me; they could have passed as me or Gigi. There were aspects about each of them that was a little off, the hair color of one, the skin color of another. The bodies were left precariously on rocks.

"Where is this crime scene?" I asked without looking back.

"The jetties that separate the beach from the state park," one of the men offered.

"When was the last victim found?"

"Forty-eight hours ago."

I spun and met Grant's gaze.

"Is it a highly popular tourist attraction?" I asked.

"Both sides of the beach are, but most people are smart enough to stay off the sharp rocks. They're dangerous."

There might be hope. The longer the wait on visiting crime scenes, the harder it was for me to target the energy. I didn't know why that was. Hell, I couldn't even explain what made it happen; it just had ever since that group started sticking me with needles.

"If you'll please have a seat," one of the men said, and I took my seat next to Grant. "I'm Deputy Sorenson. To my left is Sheriff Gallum...." I turned my gaze to the other suit waiting for the introduction, which never came.

"We appreciate whatever help you can provide us," Sorenson said and gestured to the files in front of us.

I'd already flipped through mine and tossed it back down, more interested in the map that was labeled "Last seen" with numbers 1-5 circled on it.

"He doesn't abduct from the same place twice?"

"No."

"He's calculated and smart."

"Miss Bray ..."

"Doctor," Ford, our group fancy pants, corrected, and my gaze swung to his. Interesting.

"Dr. Bray, do you have any idea who would do this?"

I rose from my seat, walked to the board, and grabbed one of the less demeaning pictures off the board. I set it on the table and then proceeded to lift my shirt up on the side just beneath my bra. "Someone who has seen this."

The tattoo in the photo was almost an exact match to the flowered birthmark both my sister and I shared.

"Do you tend to sleep around, Dr. Bray?" unidentified suit man asked.

"I'm sorry, who are you?"

His brows dipped. "Jack Sloan. My niece was one of the victims. This is my assistant, Susan Montgomery."

The assistant gave an awkward wave.

"In full disclosure, I have a sexual appetite that would rival anyone's at this table. I'm no prude, yet I know all of my partners. The problem here is that my twin has an identical mark. I'm not sure this killer is trying to make his victims look like me or her."

"Potayto, potahto," one of the deputies said.

"Hardly, gentlemen." I chuckled. "My sister and I are as different as night and day in every way other than looks. Who the killer is fixated on will tell us a lot about who he is and what he wants."

"So, bring her in," Sloan said, crossing his arms over his chest. "You two can make a list, and let's hope we have time to track them all down before spring break is over."

I felt Grant tense beside me. His jaw ticked, and I knew I had seconds before Grant exploded. He didn't do it often, but when he did, it was a matter of ducking for cover. "My sister is in a coma. I can assure you she's the angel of our duo and happens to be Grant's wife, so please be respectful, or I can just as easily return to the psych ward where they plucked me from and let you guys figure it out."

"You're a resident of a psych ward?" Susan gawked. Confusion riddled her face.

"I would let you see my nifty tracking device, but you'd have to ask Special Agent Roth to release the locking mechanism." I wiggled my arm.

"Not happening, Lucy," Agent Roth answered. "Let's focus, people."

"Now, Mrs. Bray ..." Sheriff Gallum said, rising to his feet.

"Doctor," the others around me corrected.

Sheriff Gallum pursed his lips. "Dr. Bray. I'm sure there was no ill intention in Mr. Sloan's words toward you or your sister. We just need a starting point. We now know it's someone who has seen you with...less clothes. It doesn't mean you were naked. You could have had a Peeping Tom looking in your window. It could have just as easily been at a pool party. How do you suggest we attack this?"

"That's simple. First, we'll try the crime scene, where I'll attempt a connection. If that doesn't work, or, heck, even if it does, we use me as bait. I'm guessing since he's going to all these lengths to make these women look like me or my sister that he'll go straight for the real thing if he can find it."

"And how do you suppose we let him know you're in town without going to the media and causing mass hysteria?"

I pointed to the next location he'd hit on the map, and both Sloan and I spoke at the same time. "Bar Wars."

"You've both determined a pattern?" Noah asked.

"It was in a brochure I read at the hotel. Bars on different nights are offering discounts. A new bar every night to drink cheap and the abductions fit the pattern." I answered.

"This could work," Sheriff Gallum said, and the others broke out in conversation around how it would play out.

I ignored them all again. It was going to play out however I could plan it in my head. I rose from the table and stepped over to the photos of the victims again.

These women might look like me, but they each told me something about the killer. I changed the pictures around in order of who had been first and who'd been last.

"How did you determine the pictures weren't in chronological order?" Sloan asked.

"He's getting more violent with each kill," I answered. "First one was a single stab wound. Each girl has more injuries. They were sliced and diced. The cuts are angry, not precision, and each new girl has more of them. His violence and anger toward these women are growing." I paused when I got to Sloan's relative. "I'm sorry for your loss."

"She was adopted into the family. Out of all of these girls, how did you come to pick this one as the one I'm related to? We don't even look alike." he asked.

"I could feel your sadness as I went down the list. It tripled when I got to number 3."

"I'm sorry, he said, turning to face me. "How could you feel my sadness?"

"I'm afraid that's classified," Noah said, stepping between us. "Lucy, it's time we leave. We've got to work out the logistics for your evening out."

"I'll do whatever you want, Yoda, as long as I can have a glass of wine."

"Afraid not, this isn't a vacation."

"You find this bastard, and I'll buy you a whole damn vineyard, Dr. Bray." Sloan's stony expression held my gaze.

"Mr. Sloan, I can assure you that I'll use everything in my arsenal to make that happen regardless of the wine." I nodded and turned back to Noah. "I'm going to need to go shopping."

"Why is that?" Noah asked, and I could feel Sloan's eyes boring into me.

I turned back to the board. "He has a fixation with red. Every one of these women was wearing red. That isn't a coincidence. If I had to guess, it was the similarities that drew him in, and then something about the red color sealed the deal."

She traced her fingertip over the shiny photo closest to her. These poor women were in their prime. Their futures snuffed out. Their family and friends would never know what they could have become. Anger stirred stronger in my gut. This prick was mine.

"I'm guessing that we're dealing with someone younger, who views me in his mind as his equal and the object of his affection. I need to portray the fantasy he's concocted in his mind."

8

Heat barreled down on us from the scorching afternoon sun high in the cloudless sky. Waves crashed against the shore and lapped against the jagged rocks. The soft white sand glistened beneath my feet. Each step sank further, giving my calves a long overdue workout.

The beach was packed with gobs of partygoers on one side of the rocks, and on the state park side, it was more of a family feel. Rocks lined the park side, corralling the children into water that looked no deeper than a kiddie pool. I shielded my eyes from the sun as I glanced around. "This dumping site doesn't make sense."

"Shock value," Grant said. "Families on one side, college kids on the other. More bang for his buck."

Something struck me as just a little off. Why here? "Does the state park have security?"

"Yes," Sloan answered. "One agent at the gate collecting entrance fees, one primarily dealing with the campgrounds, and two by the beach."

"He's proving how smart he is," Ford said, appearing by my side. "Even the smartest criminals need to feed their egos."

"Isn't that how we caught you?" Roth said as he passed to the rocks.

My gaze lifted to Rain. "You and I are alike?"

"We're all innocent until proven guilty, but still, I don't leave people in comas."

"You would if it was your family he screwed with," I said and moved to the rocks. I wasn't here to make friends. God knew I didn't need any additional pressure points. I already had two, and that had landed me in a psych ward.

"Now what?" Agent Roth asked. He'd never seen me work before. He didn't know what I needed, but Grant did.

"Now I work." I sat in the sand and took off my shoes, and Grant did the same. He handed me the picture of where one of the bodies had been found, but he needn't have bothered. I could see the darkened dried blood stain on one of the rocks.

He rose and offered me his hand, pulling me from the sand. We approached the rocks, and he hopped up on one before helping me. "We're doing this nice and slow."

I climbed up on the rocks and slowly took my time trying to get to the bloodstained one. With each step, I pulled energy from fishermen that used the rocks as their little honey spots to fish from. The rocks were cold beneath our feet contrasting the heat on her shoulders.

"You have any idea who this maniac could be?" Grant

asked, glancing over his shoulder at the others we'd left at the shoreline.

"No, but when I do, promise me that if I'm pulled from the case, you'll stop him. This is personal, Grant, as personal as Carl." Sweat beaded my brow and ran down my back, making my shirt stick to me. The ocean breeze did little to cool me. Not when I was already picking up the trail.

He paused and glanced back at me. "This time give me his name, and I'll take care of it."

I eased around him to the stone in question. I squatted, trying to keep my precarious balance.

"You remember what to do?"

I nodded and closed my eyes, resting my hand in the stain to pick up on the energies. Sorting through them like strands of spaghetti until I found the one with just enough sadistic anger. I latched hold of that feeling, taking it in and memorizing the vibration.

It thrummed through my veins. That was the worst part. I inhaled it like a drug, absorbing the evil to the point where I, too, was ready to kill. That was the price I paid. The reason I stayed connected to these maniacs until death occurred. The government kept that little side effect secret to themselves. Now I'd be bonded. I'd be able to connect to this killer with no way to turn it off.

When I quit fighting the need to protect myself, the anger absorbed into my mind, and a scene took place behind my closed eyes.

"Tell me what you see, Red," Grant prodded.

"His anger is consuming him," I offered, staying in his mind to watch what he did. "He tossed her on the rocks like a sack of potatoes. She doesn't appear to be dead yet, but she's close. I think she's unconscious."

My breath quickened when I saw the knife in his hands. My hand flew to my mouth. "He stabbed her in the heart and twisted the knife."

It took everything I had not to open my eyes and break the connection. I repeated everything I was seeing.

"She's dead, and he just sliced her throat. It's overkill," I whispered and continued to watch. "She wasn't wearing the necklace identical to mine. He had it in his pocket and shoved it into her mouth. He's wiping his blade on her cheek."

The killer leaned down to whisper into the dead woman's ear. "Welcome to Paradise, Lucy. I've been expecting you."

My breath hitched as fear riddled my body. My eyes flew open, and I struggled to breathe.

"Lucy, are you okay?"

I shook my head. "It was almost identical to Carl. He knew I was watching. He spoke to me."

"That's not possible," Grant argued. "Carl is still in his coma."

I quickly rose from the spot. "I'm telling you, it's identical. If it's not him, we have a copycat that knows government secrets. How the hell do you explain that?"

"Did you view from her perspective?"

"I couldn't. She wasn't emitting any feelings to latch onto. I got only his," I answered, making my way down the rocks and back into the sand.

"Well?" Agent Roth asked.

"You didn't tell me that he shoved the necklace down

their throats, but one thing is certain. He knows what I can do. He's been expecting me."

I crossed my arms over my chest. "What else aren't you guys telling me?"

"Was it Lyndsey you witnessed?" Sloan asked.

I dropped my arms and nodded. "She was unconscious when he stabbed her in the heart with the knife and twisted. She wouldn't have felt it."

The fine lines of Sloan's face remained unchanged. If that knowledge comforted him or not, he didn't say. "I'll tell her parents."

I plopped down in the sand and put my shoes on while the others talked around me. I closed my eyes as I tried, trying my best to think of something much happier.

Another scene appeared behind my eyelids. Me sitting in the sand putting on my shoes. The others standing around me. "He's here."

I slowly rose, keeping my eyes shut. I turned in the direction he'd be standing.

"He's here," I repeated, opening my eyes, locking my gaze on a man wearing a helmet sitting on a crotch rocket motorcycle.

"God damn it. He's here watching us," I growled before I took off in a flat-out run. My arms pumped and my calf muscles screamed as I plowed through the sand. The others followed behind me until we reached the asphalt.

Sloan had pulled a gun out and aimed at the suspect. He was so focused he didn't see the car transporting a family of three about to pull between his gun and the fleeing motorcycle. I shoved his gun down to point at the asphalt seconds before he pulled the trigger and the motorcycle was cut from our view by a minivan.

His labored breathing slowed as anger covered his face. "I had the shot."

"Innocents were in your way."

He shoved the gun back into its holster.

A gun that I hadn't even noticed he had. "Who the hell are you?"

I didn't wait around for an answer. I started running again, this time cutting through the trees.

Jumping over downed limbs, I ran without stopping, busting out through the trees just in time to see the motorcycle pop a wheelie out the gate. Damn it.

9

I'd missed him by a hair. I rested my palms on my knees in an attempt to catch my breath. Noah stepped out of the tree line and grabbed my hand, pulling me backward two steps. He lifted my wrist, and we both watched as the light slowly quit flashing.

"I thought you said I had ten miles," I growled.

"You are ten miles," he answered. "The other requirement was that you stay with one of us. If you go out of bounds, all bets are off, and it's barbeque time."

Noah led me back to the parking lot, where the sheriff was on his phone barking orders.

Ford approached, shoving his hands into his pockets. "Well, aren't you just full of surprises."

"You're obviously not a cop. Tell me why you're here again?"

"My expertise might come in handy."

"And what might that be?"

"I wouldn't be a man of mystery if you knew all of my

secrets," he said with a wink while he headed back to our SUV.

I hated this place already. I hated the anger coursing through my veins and the remnants of its heady hold. I needed a punching bag. Some way to drain this thick black tar-like energy of emotions raging through my body. I'd been worried I wouldn't get a bead on this killer. I'd been worried the energy was gone.

I'd been wrong.

When we arrived at the suite, Sam had his computers hooked up and was sitting idly behind them. He tapped his foot against the ground while he tossed a mixture of popcorn and M&Ms from the same bowl into his mouth.

"I already tracked the motorcycle through street cameras. I lost visual just over the bridge where the construction starts. There were no cameras operational to pick up his trail."

Well, that explained why Sam was in our little party.

"Lucy needs her shot, Carson," Roth said in passing.

Carson Tines was the quiet one of our little group, although I'd guess he was more deadly than the rest. As a medic and weapons expert, he wasn't one to be trifled with.

"How do they know about the government meds?" I asked Grant.

"We know everything, Dr. Bray." A man I hadn't met stepped out of one of the rooms. Muscles bulged in his arms. His short military haircut did little to hide the scar on his face. His dark sunglasses hid his eyes.

"And just who are you?" I asked.

"You can call me Hunt or, as you so affectionately referred to me yesterday, the puppeteer. I'm the man running this show and pulling the strings."

"Great," I said with a smile and held out the killer bracelet on my arm. "Maybe you can explain to Special Agent Roth that harming inmates is against my civil rights."

"Like the rights you took from Carl Chisolm?"

"The difference between me and Carl is that I didn't leave him for dead. I can rectify that if you'd like."

Hunt crossed his arms over his chest. "Is that you talking, or is that this new killer's rage you tapped into from the crime scene?" Hunt's jaw ticked. "Yes, Dr. Bray, I know all about you and the government experiments."

I snapped my mouth closed. He was right, and that pissed me off just about as much as needing meds to help bring me down from my evil-induced high. "If you're all out of meds, a punching bag will do. Any of you want to volunteer to spar?"

Just as the question left my lips, I felt the prick of a needle in my neck, and the world around me started to blur.

"Easy, Red. I've got you," Grant announced, wrapping his arm around my waist and leading me to my bedroom. "Just rest a bit."

I'd barely made it to the bed when the darkness sucked me back into its fold.

I was in the darkness like normal. Only a single light over-

head pointed down on me. A cage of iron bars surrounded me. Carl was on the other side. Excitement radiated out of his eyes. Motorcycle Man was standing next to him, still wearing a helmet, as Carl laughed.

"Are you surprised, Lucy?" Carl asked.

I swallowed down the bile rising in my throat. "So, you are involved?"

"I've got so many more surprises waiting for you, my dear. You haven't a clue."

I clenched my fists, ready to strike. "Who's your unlucky friend, Carl?" I turned my gaze to Motorcycle Man. "Afraid of being original, are you? Carl tried to kill my sister once. Are you so pathetic that you have to dress others up to look like me?"

I didn't get a response. Not even a groan.

"Patience, Lucy. He's waited for this moment. It won't be long now."

I laughed and gripped the bars. "Remove the cage and we can do this here and now, unless you are spineless."

Motorcycle Man slammed his fists on the cage, getting in my face. My own reflection stared back at me in the mirrored visor.

"You'll get your chance." The words were a whisper.

10

I stared down at the red dress, running my hand down the silk that hung from my shoulders. The dress had just enough class and sexiness that I knew instantly that Grant didn't buy it.

"Whose responsible for the threads?" I asked into the wire strapped inside my bra as I headed into the club.

"You're welcome, Doctor," Ford answered as he passed me, heading to the entrance with Grant beside him. Two guys going for beers wouldn't stand out. Me in this dress was sure to do the trick.

A quick glance around the parking lot and I spotted the undercover cops. I shook my head. "You need to tell the undercovers to stand down. I made them in less than a minute. We don't want to scare Motorcycle Man away before he even makes it to the door."

"Damn it," Noah growled.

"I'll be playing God tonight. I've got your location, Dr. Red." Sam, the IT guy, announced in my ear. "Stay in the safety zones where I can follow you on camera."

"Aw. You already gave me pet name." I glanced up at the camera near the bouncer at the door and blew a kiss. Sam had hacked the security system with a few strokes of the keyboard after Ford had broken in to hook up the connection to the feed.

Grinning at the bouncer, I handed over my ID and some money and, in return, got a stamp on my hand that only glowed in ultraviolet light.

"I'm in," I announced, heading up the wooden ramp to the stages and drinking areas outside the doors to the main club inside.

This club had five bar areas, three dance floors, and a band playing live music outside on the deck. It was a huge place. A place where someone might get lost.

If we'd waited another two nights, the bar hosting Bar Wars would have been smaller; easier to trace and lock on our target. This was one big crapshoot, but knowing that Motorcycle Man knew I was in town, I was betting that he'd approach. His ego would require him to make contact, just to prove he could get close.

I yanked the door open to the club and the darkness where rodents liked to hang out.

The music blared with punishing beats, rattling my bones and teeth.

The stench of sweat from bodies gyrating in unison crowded every square inch of the club. With each step I took, the sticky floor tried to keep my shoe. The overbearing smell of beer and vomit brought back memories from my sorority days.

I pressed on, gyrating my body toward the people hovering near the bar.

I closed my eyes. The same pulsing beats and beachy décor hovered in my mind behind my closed lids. I took a single deep breath and opened my eyes again. A smile slid onto my face.

He was here.

"It's time to play, people. He's here."

I made my way up to the bar and winked at the bartender. He slowly made his way down to me, his gaze lowering to my chest. "What can I get you, sexy?"

"Glass of white wine."

"Lucy, you and I discussed drinking." Roth's voice rasped in my ear. I ignored him, just like I ignored most men in my life.

"Ease up, Noah. If the killer has his way, this might be the last thing I ever drink."

"If you drink that, your guard will be down." Grant's voice drifted into my ears.

Leave it to my brother-in-law to try to make a glass of wine sound like the worst choice I could make. When the bartender returned with my glass of wine, I slid my money over to him. He slid a napkin with his name and number. I smiled as I picked up the glass and met Grant's gaze as I sipped.

"If he thinks that I'm drinking, he'll be more prone to approach." I always had a plan, and this was mine. He was going to need to think that I was vulnerable. How did I know? Because I would've done the same thing. I closed my eyes for a brief moment, trying to figure out if I could get the direction from which the killer was watching me. When I opened my eyes again, it was hard for me to pinpoint with any accuracy given the sea of people.

I turned my back to the bar and glanced up at the VIP area. I spotted Sloan behind the red rope. His assistant, Susan, was hanging on his arm. She'd ditched the office clothes and was now dressed in something sexier than even I was wearing. She whispered into his ear before turning her gaze at me.

"Sloan is here in the VIP area." Static filled my earpiece, and there was no response. Was the killer jamming our connection?

I hadn't even pondered the idea further when a hand smacked my ass, and I turned toward the tall guy standing behind me. He was in his mid-twenties, had dark hair and a fuck-me smile. He didn't say a word as his hands traveled up to my hips and he began to sway from side to side. He leaned in to whisper in my ear.

"Are you ready for me to rock your world?"

It took everything I had not to roll my eyes and worse. I smiled up at him and pulled his head closer to mine. "Actually yes. You're just the man I need."

The guy chuckled and pulled me closer, his body swaying against mine. "I'm going to make you crave me."

As if. The static in my ear cleared. "Is he your target?" Noah asked in my ear.

I closed my eyes, unable to determine the killer's surroundings. All I knew was he wasn't staring across the room at me with hunger in his eyes like the guy who had me in his hold. I wouldn't indulge, but I could. A grin settled on my lips as I shook my head, leading the stranger to the dance floor, leaving my wine glass on the railing.

"Hi, I'm..."

I held my finger to his lips. "Your name doesn't matter," I said, running my hands over his hard body. "Only this does."

"Hell yeah," he said and tossed his arms up the air when I turned, giving him my back, and began to grind into him.

"Lucy, you are not here on vacation. Lose the guy."

I squatted, going low, and spoke into my speaker. "This is better. Trust me. This will save us time."

I held Sloan's gaze above as I ran my hands down my body. He'd headed toward the stairs when the woman he was with stepped in his way. I couldn't hear her words, but there was little doubt she was talking about me as she pointed in my direction.

Ignoring her, he stepped around her and headed down the stairs. I gave him a slow shake of my head, but that didn't stop him.

I muttered out a string of cuss words as Sloan crossed the dance floor. He was going to ruin everything.

As if I'd made it happen with the power of my thoughts, Sloan moved into the college guy's way and placed his own hands on my waist, drawing me into his hold.

"Dude, she was dancing with me." College guy growled and shoved against Sloan's chest. Sloan didn't budge.

I left them both standing on the dance floor and headed back to the bar to get another glass of wine. Speaking to myself, knowing the others could hear me, I said, "College guy is the better choice. He's a douche and won't be viewed as a threat, whereas Sloan is like a fucking brick wall. Noah, handle your men," I growled as I held up a twenty and waved it at the bartender.

"He would, but I'm not his to handle," Sloan said, sliding up to the bar between me and another person waiting. His hand rested on my waist as he leaned into me. "If you're meaning to make the killer jealous, I'll do that faster. Watch and learn."

He lifted me up into the air, and I wrapped my legs around his waist as he crashed his lips to mine. Heat seared through my veins as he moved to press me up against a nearby wall. His tongue dueled with mine as his palms squeezed my butt cheeks. Heat pooled between my thighs when he finally came up for breath. He stared at me, intent in his eyes.

"If he's here, and the jealous type, he's about to blow a gasket."

My heart raced as I stared into his eyes. He slowly lowered me back to my feet. The hem of my dress slowly inched up my thighs until Sloan lowered it. He took me by the hand and led me back to the dance floor.

"The college kid would have been easy pickings. You, on the other hand..."

"Are going to get you all hot and bothered and then piss you off, where you hit me. He's going to think you're not only emotionally off balanced but physically unstable, too, when I stop your punch in mid-air. You'll be pissed and ripe for the picking."

I stared up into his eyes as my body swayed with his. His plan had potential. Rough around the edges, but still potential.

"You know I'm right. Better me, who knows the score, than the college kid, Lucy. Wouldn't you agree?"

"Lucy, it's your call," Noah said in my ear, reminding me we had an audience.

"It could work," I said.

11

Sloan leaned into me and lowered his head. "It will work, but we have to make him believe it," he said as he sucked my ear lobe into his mouth.

I closed my eyes and grinned. That was one thing I could do.

The killer's anger grew over the next hour. I could feel him as if he were standing next to me. He was buying it, and why wouldn't he? Sloan had me on the brink of believing it myself. In another life, in another moment, I'd act on the heat we generated. We were like the sparking wick of a Roman candle on the verge of taking flight.

The sultry heat dampened my forehead. My satin dress was clinging to my body. I waved my hand over my face in an attempt to cool myself. Sloan took me by the hand and led me to the bar. He took the stool and pulled me to stand between his legs. "Wine?"

"Water," I answered, grabbing a napkin and dotting at

the makeup on my face. I could only imagine the kind of clown I looked like.

I took the bottle and downed it, almost finishing the entire thing before I gasped for air.

He watched. The heat in his eyes left little doubt that he was fighting the part he was playing. He wanted me.

"I need the restroom," I said, tossing my napkins into the trash and heading toward the neon sign.

I pushed open the door into the bathroom to find two coeds standing at the sinks. One was swiping lipstick on her lips as she bobbled, fighting the liquor in her system and gravity from taking hold. The other, with her hands stuck in her shirt, plumped up her boobs in her bra. Stalls lined the walls, two with closed doors and the last with its door hanging askew. The overwhelming stench of liquor and sweat filled the tiny room. I guess that was better than the alternative. It might be midnight, but it was too early for these partygoers to be feeling the effects and getting sick everywhere.

I grabbed some paper towels as I stared in the aged mirror speckled with water spots. The overhead lights flickered. My eyeliner had started to raccoon around my eyes. My skin was flushed from dancing. No way would I give Sloan credit. I wiped the paper towel beneath my raccoon eyes to fix the smudges before tossing it into the trashcan and grabbing another. I dotted the sweat from my body as the other girls slurred their words, talking about the guys they were taking home.

No matter how much this room reeked and differed from the OCD-clean bathroom at Camp Cupcake, I'd still choose this one. Freedom trumped sparkling floors.

I slipped into a stall and locked the door. I needed a minute to myself. Just a minute to forget how my life had turned out. I closed the toilet lid and sat down on it, resting my face in my hands. How had it come to this? One wrong choice in the name of science and my life had never been the same since.

The girls giggled again as their heels clicked the tiles. The loud club noise was brief, suggesting the girls had left me alone.

"Make it quick, Lucy. We can't watch you in the bathroom." Noah's urgency wasn't at the top of my list of concerns.

"Copy that," I answered anyway. Otherwise, he'd send someone in to check on me.

The loud club music invaded my space again as someone entered. Minutes ticked by without the sound of a flushing toilet or faucet being turned on. A pair of men's shoes stood in front of my stall.

"This is the ladies' room," I called out.

The feet began to move, and the music flared again as the person left.

"Lucy, you all right?" Grant asked.

"I'm fine," I answered, flipping the lock and yanking the door open.

Fear clogged my throat as I read the lipstick-written words left on the aged mirror.

Have your fun, Lucy. I've been having mine.

The words didn't scare me until my gaze dropped to the music box sitting on the counter. Panic escalated to defcon 5. I grabbed it and flipped it over, forgetting to breathe. My and Gigi's initials were carved into it. We each had a music box given to us on our birthday's. Only mine had our initials. This had been in my apartment, even worse, in my bedroom. I flipped the lid open to find the lipstick inside, and panic laced my spine. I keyed up the mic.

"He's been in my house and Gigi's," I shouted as I ran for the door. I yanked it open and fell into Sloan's waiting arms.

"Did you see a man come through here?" I asked, glancing up and down the hall.

"No," he answered. "What's wrong?"

"He was in the bathroom. He's been inside my home," I screamed as I shoved passed him and pushed open the only other door in the hallway.

The men's restroom was worse than the women's, with three urinals standing on the wall and only one stall.

I glanced beneath the stall to find a pair of men's dress shoes. Anger stirred my gut.

"I've got you now, fucker," I said as I kicked the door from the hinges.

A woman squealed as she clung to the man's chest. Her skirt was bunched around her hips. The collar of her shirt dragged below her bustline. His pants hung around his legs.

"Sorry." I apologized as heat claimed my cheeks. I pulled the door back as best I could. Sloan took me by the arm and led me out.

Grant and Ford hurried down the hall in my direction. Grant took me by the arms and looked me over. "You okay?"

I nodded with shaking limbs. "He's been in my house and yours."

I handed him the music box. "Grant, go to Gigi. She needs you more than me. Go make sure she's okay."

I watched as his head and heart warred with his needs. "Leave or I will, Grant. I'll call this off and do something stupid to send us all packing."

12

"Lucy, Gigi is fine. I've got her tucked away at another hospital under a fake name. He hasn't found her. He couldn't have."

I yanked the lipstick out of the music box and held it up to show him. Gigi was the name of the color, and the only one my sister wore. Her friend in the cosmetics industry had made it special and named it after her. "Grant, don't make me do this the hard way."

Noah appeared in the hallway. Anger radiated in the narrow space. "Grant, go check on your wife. If he doesn't take a girl from here, we've got two days before he hits again."

"Why two days? I thought Bar Wars was nightly."

"The next club on the list is closed for renovations. We passed it on the way here. The brochure must be outdated."

"Who's to say he's going to stick to his pattern?" Grant said, slamming his palm against the wall. "Do you have any idea what Gigi would do to me if she knew that the killer was that close to Lucy and I didn't stay to watch out after her?"

I slowly nodded. I understood now. His pain and anger ran as deep as mine did. I took his hand and stared into his eyes. "You saw what I did to Carl. I can take care of myself. You go take care of her. If anything happens to her, it would kill us both."

He nodded and handed me back the music box.

"I've already got him on a flight," Sam said in our ears.

"Sam, check the parking lot for motorcycles. Make sure there's none leaving with women on the back."

"Already done, Dr. Red Hot," Sam announced. "There were three, and only one had a woman. I'm tracking them now."

This killer was smarter than I gave him credit for. He'd been in my home, and he hadn't struck when he had the chance in the bathroom. He was calculating and in control. That changed everything.

In the daze of my own spinning mind, I followed the others out of the club and back to the SUV and van parked next to it. The door flew open, and Sam grinned down at me.

"Let me know next time you want to go dancing. I'll be your partner." Sam wiggled his brows.

I frowned and slipped inside the SUV to wait on the others while I worked a psychological profile in my head. Something was wrong with what I was working with. His age and the way his killings had escalated were in complete contrast to that stunt in the bathroom. He wasn't just a cocky killer. He was a psychotic stalking mastermind. Those were two very opposite variables.

The ride back to the hotel was slow with college kids cruising and hanging out of cars flirting with one another. The moon shined high in the night sky. I closed my eyes, searching for his emotional strings that would take me to him. Nothing.

Damn him. Damn me.

The hotel was brimming with people; only they weren't the vibrant sparkling-eyed kids from earlier who'd been just heading out for a fun night out. These guys were dragging in, propping each other up, and barely able to function.

We all stepped onto the elevator. My shoulders sagged as I leaned against the wall. This wasn't how it was supposed to end. My music box was clutched tight in my hand digging the hinges into my palms. I glanced up to find the rest of my bunkmates staring at me.

"He got in my head," I said, not caring if they understood. "He threw me off my game."

"You're human." The words were as much of a surprise as the deep voice they came from. Carson, our resident weapons expert, had broken into my pity-party. "Roth, she needs to be armed. Either with your consent or without, she's not going back into the field unable to defend herself."

"Aw, that's sweet. You thought I was vulnerable." I nudged his shoulder. Reaching down into my dress and into my bra, I pulled out a switchblade and handed it to him. "Compliments of the college kid who couldn't keep his hands off my ass."

Carson's gaze held mine, his stone veneer intact and

unmoving. He took the knife and flicked it open. "This will do for now."

He slapped it closed and was about to hand it back when Roth intercepted my bounty. "What part of dangerous psych ward patient are you guys not understanding? She doesn't get to play with weapons, especially knives, not after the way she sliced up Carl."

"She could gut us in our sleep," Ford said as the elevator dinged and we all stepped out.

"Now why would I do that? You're my ride home," I said, bypassing Ford and stepping into our suite. I headed to the bedroom and changed into sleep shorts and a tank top before going out on the balcony to claim a seat.

The ocean breeze made goosebumps rise on my arms. The sound of crashing waves below was a melody that I'd replay in my mind when I was back at sleepover camp. The psych ward wasn't as horrible as prison, not when I could predict what the doctors and patients were going to do. I compared it to a walk in the park and totally worth the torture I'd inflicted.

The sliding glass door behind me slid open, and Ford stepped out, carrying a plate with pizza and a beer. "It's not wine, but it's liquor."

"Thanks," I said, taking it from him. He returned seconds later with his own.

"So, are you out here plotting how to kill us in our sleep?" Ford asked as I sipped my beer.

I grinned. "Not yet. I was just out here thinking that this guy got in my mind. That was unexpected. I underestimated him."

"That's half the battle, isn't it? Trying to figure out

what makes a person tick. Sometimes people are easy to peg; other times, it's like shooting an arrow at a brick wall. But I can tell you that the best way that I've learned to read people is by seeing the way they live. You can tell a lot about a person by the way they keep their home." He shrugged. "Or don't keep their home."

I took a bite of pizza. "You sound like you're talking from experience. So, remind me again. What is it that you do?"

He glanced over his shoulder before leaning in. "I'm a thief. There isn't a lock that can keep me out or a room and building that I can't breach. I didn't start that way. I was a squatter, believe it or not."

"Explains the pricey threads," I said, glancing at his dress pants.

"There's nothing wrong with appreciating the finer things in life, Dr. Bray."

"Lucy," I corrected him. "I was wrong about you. We aren't anything alike."

"I told you," he said, glancing at me as he dangled the pizza slice over his face. He took a bite and chewed before he continued. "This pizza isn't half bad, but it doesn't even come close to the pizza I had when I housesat at 39th Street unit 102."

I glanced in his direction and took another sip of my beer. "Explain."

"I associate food with experiences. The pizza in unit 102 was handcrafted by an old Italian woman who had flown to California to visit her children. I was sixteen when I stayed in her home. That was the night I learned the life lesson that people lie."

My brows scrunched. "How did that come about?"

His lip pulled up at the corner. "I found the empty, store-bought sauce jars in her trash. She might sell her pizza as authentic, but it was as fake as you and me."

"You would think that she'd get rid of the evidence before asking you to housesit."

He chuckled. "I didn't house-sit; I squatted."

"You call it squatting; I call it breaking and entering," I said, taking another sip of my beer. "And just think, your illusion of the old woman would still be intact if you hadn't broken the law."

"It's better to know the truth, no matter how many lies you spin. It's like a spider web that can be brought down with one wrong stroke of a broom. If I were a bad guy, just imagine what I could do with that information."

Ford and I sat silently the rest of the time on the balcony. He looked as though he'd turned inward just as I had. The voices in the pool area slowly started to dissipate as morning hours crept ever closer.

There was little in the way of evidence. These spring-breakers might not even be reported as missing until it was time to pack their things and leave. The alternate was us finding their dead bodies.

As of now, the only connection I had to the killer was in the space of our minds, and even that was limited if his emotions weren't heated enough for me to grab hold.

Around two a.m., Noah pulled us back inside and told us to hit the sack. As if sleep would ever come that easily. I was almost afraid to close my eyes, afraid of the monsters I might find. The ones that threatened to destroy me every day.

13

I woke to the knock at the door. Wiping the sleep from my eyes, I crawled out of bed and went to answer. Noah was standing on the other side, bright-eyed and dressed and ready for the day. He held a cell phone out for me to take. "Grant wants to talk to you."

I slipped the phone up to my ear. "You got her?"

"Yes, your sister is fine, although you were right about one thing. He has been in both of our houses."

I shouldn't be surprised. "This guy isn't a typical serial killer, and he's not a typical stalker. He's somewhere in between."

"I don't care what he is. He's fixated with either you or Gigi, and we have to put a stop to it."

I squeezed my eyes closed and rubbed the bridge of my nose. "Grant, if he knows where we live, there's a good chance he knows which hospital you put Gigi in. I need you to stay there with her."

The line went silent. I could always hear the war waging in his mind. I didn't have to be psychic or connected to him to know that he was having a hard time deciding. "You stay; I've got this."

"Lucy, I have always had your back. Who's going to have it if I'm not there?"

I stared up into Roth's eyes debating if I could trust him. "There are plenty of men here to keep me safe. I need Gigi to have at least one. I'll keep you posted, and if anything should change, I promise to let you know. Take care of her, Grant. I'm counting on you."

"You know I will," Grant said. "Keep me posted; I can be on a flight out of town and back to Florida within hours."

"Give her a hug for me. Don't worry. I'll steal somebody's phone later and call you with an update." I chuckled as I handed Noah back his phone. His would be the one that I took.

I stepped around Noah and headed for the kitchen. Sam was already behind his computer desk, his foot tapping, his mind totally into whatever he was doing. My steps slowed as I entered the kitchen. Sloan was leaning against the counter with a coffee cup in hand. "Who let you in?"

"I have friends in high places."

I understood Sloan's need to be involved in this case. It was personal for him, just as Carl had been personal for me. He wanted to make sure justice was served, and I couldn't blame him. Although Sloan wouldn't deliver the fatal blow. This killer, this stalker, he was as fixated on me as I was now on him. I didn't care who helped me reach my objective, whether it was Sloan, Noah, or Ford. Each man served their purpose, and I'd be a fool not to recognize it.

"So, you're just along for the ride to see that I get things done?"

"You could say that."

"Whatever secrets you're hiding, if this affects Noah's merry team of misfits, make no mistake that you and I are going to go rounds."

The clacking of fingers on the keyboard paused. Sam inhaled a sharp breath. The computer geek wasn't like the other men. His only objective was to provide assistance and make sure that we had it. I liked him best.

"I think I've got something."

I poured my coffee, turned my back to Sloan, and left the kitchen crossing the living room to where Sam sat. Stepping around his computer there were three pictures on the screen. One was a woman in a red dress on the back of a motorcycle. The date and time stamp were from last night. Sam pointed to the intricate design on the dress. "I went back through all of the footage, and I know who this woman is." He pointed to the other two pictures. "I found her when she was paying her cover charge, and I zoomed in on the ID. Then I did a search of the woman's financials and learned that she paid for a hotel room up the road. After hacking the hotel's computer log, I discovered she never used her card key last night. If you're going to find her alive, maybe you should check with the college kids she traveled with staying next door."

"If you know what the guy on the motorcycle was wearing, can't you do the same thing with him?"

"Do you know how many men were wearing blue jeans and black shirts?"

"I don't have any idea. Maybe half the guys last night."

"You'd be mistaken." Sam's fingers clicked on the keyboard a few more times, and several faces stared back at me. "Forty guys were wearing the exact same thing. I've eliminated thirty-five of them for one reason or another. Some weren't even in town when the first killing happened. I'm in the process of crossing the remaining five faces at the other bars where the abductions occurred." A few more clicks of the keyboard and the five remaining faces flared back at us.

"Do you recognize any of them?" Sloan asked.

I didn't have a memory like Ford had for the places he'd stayed or the lessons he'd learned. I didn't recognize any of these people. "No, but at least one of them must've been in my life."

"Maybe it ticked him off that you didn't even notice him," Sloan said.

"If you can get me some names from their ID's they showed to get into the club, we can pull credit cards, or hell, even check social media to see where they're all staying. Once we have that I'll go have a chat with each of them." I said.

"You might want to get dressed first," Noah said from across the room. "Run each name and find a local home address as well. One of these guys has crossed path with either Lucy or Gigi, and assuming neither one of them had been on vacation, they had to have crossed paths closer to Lucy's and Gigi's homes. Not to mention he knows where they live."

"That's right!" Excitement drummed through my veins. "I've only been incarcerated for six months. He had to have been in my home during that time to get the music box. The worst-case scenario is pulling traffic cams from the light that turns into my subdivision. There are thirty-five houses in my subdivision, and I'm sure that would be a menial task for an exceptional hacker like you to pull the vehicle makes and models and eliminate each one as it turns in."

Sam grinned. "You think I'm exceptional?"

I kissed his cheek. "I'm just glad you're on our team. Get us those addresses while I go change."

14

I brushed my teeth and opted for a quick shower, hurrying to get ready. Today might be the day when we actually caught this creep. I'd just stepped out of the shower and left the bathroom with the towel still wrapped around my body when the adjoining door opened.

Ford's gaze slowly slid down my body. His jaw ticked as he stood stock-still until his gaze met mine. The friendly man from last night on the balcony had turned into something more somber.

"I should've knocked," Ford said, stepping into the bathroom.

My hand was on the doorknob. "I might've invited you in."

I slowly closed the bathroom door and continued to get ready. This might be over in no time, but I'd be damned if I didn't have a little bit of fun while away from the cuckoo's nest.

I met the others back in the living room. They had a

map out and had circled places on it. Sam was behind the computer. He'd just tossed some popcorn into his mouth before he started to choke, quickly rising from his seat. He pointed at the screen. I walked over to him, picked up his soda, and handed it to him. Turning toward the screen, I now understood what had caught him off guard. A crotch rocket just like the one I'd seen before was sitting outside one of the addresses. We had just narrowed this down from five people to one.

"What's that address?"

Sam sputtered and tried to clear his throat before he could speak. "That's downtown Panama City near the marina," he said.

"I call dibs on that location," I said, slipping into my shoes.

"We came as one unit. We will check each address as one unit. We aren't breaking apart the team," Noah said.

He was probably right; it was safer that way, if not as effective.

I glanced around the room to find Sloan missing just as the suite door clicked closed. It took only a second for me to figure out that Sloan was going after him by himself. He wanted a head start. I ran to the door and tossed it open to find Sloan pressing the elevator call button. I stomped down the hall.

"You're going to take this away from me?"

"I'm not taking anything away from you, Lucy," Sloan said.

"You forget I can feel your anger. Your hate is sticking out from you like a porcupine. You want him to die, and I don't blame you, but before you aim your gun and pull the trigger, I want you to remember one thing."

"And what's that?"

"Remember where anger got me. You take a life, you give yours. Why not let me do it for you? You get your revenge, and I already have a room in Camp Cupcake. They already knew I was crazy before they brought me here. You, on the other hand, might have a different outcome and be sent to prison."

The elevator opened, and I grabbed his arm, stopping him before he could step on. "Don't do this."

"Do you realize what he took from me? I'll have to deal with that every day for the rest of my life. At every reunion, at every family occasion, my niece's face will be missing and I couldn't live with myself if I'm not the one who stops him."

I rested my palm behind his neck and pulled his lips down to mine, stepping into his hold. Our lips locked like they had on the dance floor, except without as much passion as we once shared. When the door was about to close, he stuck out his hand, stopping it, and broke the kiss.

"Under different circumstances, Lucy, you and I would've been a force to be reckoned with."

Sloan stepped onto the elevator, and I stood there watching as the doors slid closed. I turned to go back to the room to find Ford standing there. As I walked by, I slipped the keys out of my pocket and dropped them into Ford's palm.

"He only thinks he's getting to this creep first."

Ford chuckled. "You don't have any morals, do you?"

"That isn't lack of morals; that's greed," I said just as the others stepped out. They gave me a run down on my role. I would be last to enter. It was comical that these guys still considered me fragile.

Sloan was downstairs waiting by our SUV, his face taut with anger as he watched me approach. I smiled back in response and handed him back his keys. "You can follow us, or we can follow you."

"Where did you learn the art of picking someone's pocket?" Sloan asked.

"Would you believe that I learned it in the psych ward?" I shrugged passed him. I didn't care what he believed, as long as he understood that he and I were on the same team and wanted the same outcome. I didn't care if this killer lived or died, though my choice would've been the latter, considering he was targeting so many women and making them look like me and Gigi, not to mention renting space in my head.

I slid into the SUV with Ford on one side and Sloan on the other. Carson, sat shotgun, with Noah driving. Tines was supposed to be my muscle on this outing, even though I suspected that Noah could defend himself, and with Sloan, there was no question. Ford, on the other hand, could probably find an escape route for both of us quicker than the others could draw their weapons. Was that his superpower?

The underbelly of downtown Panama City was nothing like Panama City Beach, where the vibrant high-schoolers and college kids partied and merchants catered to clientele willing to spend money. From over-staffed hotels with five to ten kids deep sharing a room to the shiny restaurants offering seafood and tourist-wear.

Downtown Panama City probably used to be a vibrant place, until the hurricane came through. Structures were torn apart, yellow and pink home insulation sat on the roadside, trees had been ripped by the roots and tilted, lying on every available space. Hurricane Michael had hit almost a year ago, but several blue tarps still flailed in the wind on rooftops. The closer we got to downtown, the more despair was visible. Homeless vagrants wandered the streets, wearing dirty clothes and some without shoes. A few pushed shopping carts full of their prized possessions. My heart ached for these people, the ones the world forgot.

If I was ever set free again, these were the people that I would come back to help. These were the ones who needed it most.

The feeling of despair saturated the air in the SUV, warring only with the feeling of determination. I didn't bother trying to figure out who was feeling what as we pulled into the hotel parking lot, where the sign was lying beside the pole it had been affixed to. Half of the roof was covered in tarps; the other side of the building had vehicles parked in front of the doors.

"Which room?" I asked.

"Sam ran the motorcycle's license plate, and the occupant has room 103," Noah answered.

"First floor, easy escape," I muttered as we all climbed out.

I'd started for the door when Tines pulled me back

and shook his head. "You're to stay behind me, are we clear?"

"Clear as a cowboy on Friday night looking for a filly."

Guns were drawn, and the others proceeded to the door. Ford stayed behind with me. He grinned and tossed me Noah's keys. "Rule number 1—always have an escape plan."

"Wouldn't that defeat the purpose?" I asked, tossing him back the keys. I closed my eyes, not feeling any bit of the killer's anger. Either he'd found a way to block me or wasn't angry.

Noah returned with the hotel clerk and a door keycard. He took the key and handed it to Tines, who undid the lock.

Chaos ensued as Tines crashed into the room, followed by Noah and Sloan, yelling "Put your hands in the air." Their voices bounced off the walls.

I peeked around the doorframe and found a young guy in bed with the girl from last night. Neither were clothed, their naked bodies only covered by a sheet. Her intricate red dress lay discarded on the floor.

"Who the hell are you guys?" the guy asked.

"Your worst enemy," Noah answered. "Get dressed, kid. I'm taking you in for questioning in a series of murders."

The girl slid off the bed with the sheet and grabbed her dress, running for the bathroom.

"You got the wrong guy." The suspect slowly pulled up his jeans, holding my gaze as he zipped them. The emotions in the room were hard to decipher.

Fear on the young woman's part as she scurried out of

the bathroom. Tines grabbed her and took her outside, out of harm's way.

Anger radiated from Noah and Sloan.

But it was the kid that left me bewildered. It was almost as if I couldn't read him. Nothing, no feelings whatsoever, even though a smile slid onto his lips as he was putting on his boots.

My gaze darted around the room. There wasn't a suitcase in sight. No toiletries from where I could see beyond the open bathroom door. Noah cuffed the kid before stepping out to call the sheriff's department for a deputy to come transport this guy.

Sloan grabbed the cuffs and yanked the guy out with a force that almost made him trip.

A hungry smile played on the young kid's lips. "Even prettier today."

My brows dipped. "Seeing your stalking victim up close makes a difference. Maybe now you won't screw up the details."

His brows dipped. "Stalking victim? What the hell are you talking about? I saw you last night practically having sex on the dance floor with him."

The kid gestured toward Sloan.

Tines stepped out of the room with a wallet in hand. "Edward Gentry lives in the same town as Lucy."

Tines tossed Sloan the wallet. "That can't be a coincidence."

As they baited the kid, I opened up my feelers, trying to get a read on Gentry as I quietly studied his face. I'm not sure I'd ever seen this guy before. Had we gotten this wrong?

"What are you charging me with? Because that girl told me she was twenty-one."

"You wish that was all you were being hauled in for," Ford said.

"You're wanted as a person of interest for questioning in the Bar Wars murders."

"The what?" Gentry asked as he shook his head vehemently. "I don't even know what you're talking about. You've got the wrong guy."

Noah slid up next to me, leaning against the SUV. "Well, you getting any vibes off him? Is he our guy?"

"I'm not sure," I answered, and that was the truth. "More often than not, I can pick out a menacing person just by his emotions, but this guy, I'm not getting anything."

"So, you're saying we're wrong?" Noah asked.

"No, I'm saying that this guy must be a master manipulator. You all but charged him with murder, and most people would be scared, or pissed, or some type of emotion to tell me what's going on internally." I glanced at Noah. "This guy has nothing going on under the hood. He's either masking it, or he's really arrogant enough to believe that he'll get off the hook. I'm telling you, no emotions."

"Great," Noah murmured as the deputy pulled up and stuffed Gentry into the back seat.

We followed the deputy back to the sheriff's department, and they put Gentry in an interrogation room while the rest of us decided who was going to do the talking. Obviously, Noah had interrogation skills while Sloan was willing to beat the truth out of him. Ford looked as disinterested to be here as Tines, as they were leaning back in the conference room chairs.

"I'm the obvious choice," I said, earning everyone's stare as they turned toward me. "I'm the one he wants."

There was a chorus of no's around the room. Noah complained I didn't know how to interrogate. Tines insisted that I not be alone with Gentry. Ford just shook his head, and Sloan, well, he wasn't ready to give up the reins on his own potential to go in.

"You said Gentry wasn't feeling any emotions. How are you going to get to him?"

"Leave that to me," I said as the rest of the group followed me down the hall.

Noah handed me the file that Sam had rushed to put together. It didn't have much, except a little of his background including his father's ties to this area. Several properties including a boat slip were registered in his daddy's name.

The others went into the observation room, and I took a deep breath before I entered the room, coming face to face with Gentry.

15

"I've got nothing to say. Either charge me with something or I'm leaving."

The room was similar in size and shape to the interrogation room that I'd been in recently. A two-way mirror hung on a wall over a scarred table. Gentry sat on a battered metal chair across from another vacant one.

I still wasn't feeling anything from Gentry. Nothing. But I was hoping to change that.

I grasped the file and held it against my thighs. "You aren't under arrest; those guys just have a few questions."

"What, aren't you one of them?" he asked.

I chuckled "God, no. I'm like you. Sort of," I said, lifting my bracelet. "Only they have me tied to this tracker."

His gaze shot to the bracelet, and something quickly crossed his face. I could feel Noah's aggravation from the room next door. It was thick like honey, only less sweet.

"So what? Are you like on probation?"

"Hardly. They haven't released me, but they have asked me to help find a killer."

"Why you?" he asked.

"The girls that are dying look just like me. Do you think I'm pretty?"

"Is that a trick question?" he asked, and his gaze shot to the mirror as if looking for a response.

"No, not a trick question." I sat down as he rose.

"Let me out of here," he said straight to the two-way glass.

"You're free to go," I said and gestured to the door. "I tried to tell them that you weren't smart enough to pull this off. I mean just look at you. You're not very muscular, and it would have taken some strong muscles to get those dead girls in position."

I opened my senses in his direction, hoping that'd I'd hit a nerve. Still nothing.

He sat back down. "You don't know me...Mrs...."

"Dr. Bray, but you can call me Lucy," I said.

"Dr. Bray, I don't know what you're playing at, but there's no way I did what you think. I love women. Why would I hurt any of them?"

I propped my elbows on the table and played with the necklace around my neck. The one that the killer had a sick fascination with. "I know why I'd hurt someone, but that's just me. I don't know your reasoning."

"That's because I don't have one. I didn't do anything," he argued.

I flipped the file open to find the date he'd purchased the hotel room. "You were in town, and you're driving the same type of vehicle that's been spotted around the crime scene. It's not a long shot. You had means and opportunity. They just need motive."

His lips twitched, giving me at least something. "Let me get this straight. You think that I transported whoever this dead girl is on the back of my bike and then dumped her. Dead weight wouldn't let me maneuver turns. How do you suppose I defied the laws of gravity?"

"Another vehicle?" I offered.

I took out the picture of one of the women and laid it in front of him. "Have you seen this girl before?"

"Yes, no, maybe," he answered. "It's spring break, and what I tend to notice on these girls isn't their face."

No emotion, no anger, no nothing, not even his annoyance for being detained. It was like he knew I'd be looking for it. Wanting it, needing it to tell me if I was on the right track.

I twirled the bracelet on my arm. "So, you're not looking for a forever kind of connection, huh?"

"No." His gaze twinkled.

"Where were you three nights ago?"

He sat back in his chair and crossed his arms over his chest, letting out a sigh. "God, I don't even know. I've stayed drunk most of my vacation."

"You like to drink, and party?"

"Doesn't everyone?" he asked.

"Oh, to be young and stupid," I said whimsically.

"Dr. Bray, don't hate yourself because this town is currently full of women that have more to offer than you do. It's a college thing, and you must have finished college what...a decade ago?"

I held his gaze, not answering his question, when a

knock sounded on the door. Noah walked in, accompanied by another man in a suit carrying a briefcase. "Dr. Bray, Gentry's father's attorney is here."

"That was fast. We've had him for all of half an hour. You must have traveled at warp speed all the way from... North Carolina?" I asked.

"Yes," he answered, "and this meeting is over unless you have something to charge him with or proof he committed the crimes you're suggesting. Either arrest him or let him go."

Gentry rose from his seat. "They don't have any proof." He winked at me in passing, "Because I didn't do it."

He'd made it to the door before I called out, "Gentry."

He turned.

"I'll be seeing you," I said with a smile.

"Harassing my client won't be tolerated," the attorney said.

"Killing innocent women won't be either, Counselor. You might want to reconsider the type of criminal you're protecting." I smiled even wider.

"I thought you said you could get him to talk," Sloan said, storming into the interrogation room after Gentry and his attorney left.

"I never said I could get him to talk, but we know more now than we did before."

"Did you feel any of his emotions?" Noah asked.

"He blocked his emotions from me. That right there is telling enough. He had something to hide," I said while silently pondering how exactly he knew that he needed to block me. Did this weasel know about the secret government program?

"You didn't get him to admit to anything," Sloan said.

"I didn't have to, not yet. He knows that we're on to him. I firmly believe 100 percent, with all my heart, that this man is the killer, regardless of whether we can prove it yet. He knows I'm on to him." I waved my wrist with the bracelet on it. "He knows I'm here and that I believe he isn't as smart as others believe. He's cocky enough to try and get to me, and he knows I had a GPS tracker. That cocky son of bitch will try to outsmart you guys. I can guarantee it. We won't have to chase him around anymore; he'll come to us."

The sheriff stuck his head in the door. "Uh, I'm not so sure he's the one. We just got a call about another body, similar wounds, died within the time that you had Gentry here."

I shook my head. It wasn't possible. Gentry was the killer. I knew it, no matter what the sheriff had found. "Where'd they find the body, on the rocks, like the other girls?"

"She was found unconscious on your floor at the hotel. She didn't survive the trip to the hospital," the sheriff answered.

I met Noah's gaze. I wasn't wrong; I knew I wasn't. "Take me back to the hotel. This one is fresh and I'll connect easier."

"Your associate, Sam, called it in. He's the one who found her outside the door."

"How convenient do you think it is that we were

Gentry's alibi when this girl showed up and dropped dead in front of our hotel door?"

"Just because she died while he was here, doesn't mean he didn't commit the wounds that took her life." He could have easily taken the one girl back to the hotel, waited until she passed out before leaving in the middle of the night to inflict these wounds. He would have an alibi. This guy was smarter than any of us were giving him credit.

We stepped out of the sheriff's department building. There was a limo in the parking lot. I didn't need to see who was inside to know the identity of the person behind the tinted windows. I'd read Gentry's file. The deceased mother came from old-school money, and when she'd died, she left Gentry's father a very rich man. It was that money that paid for the attorney and property in this town. There were a lot of places we were going to have to check out to find out which one was Gentry's little hidey-hole where he was experimenting on these women. And I had every intention of doing just that.

The limo continued to sit there while the rest of us got into the SUV. The ride back to the hotel was spent in quiet contemplation. Sloan's anger and frustration were choking. Even Tines, the most laid-back of all, seemed a bit on edge with the way he rested his hand over his weapon. We parked at the hotel and spotted Sam standing on the balcony looking down on us.

Unease settled in my stomach, something I couldn't quite put my finger on. As I stepped out of the SUV, my gaze traveled over everything. Looking, searching for something in the parking lot that could explain the range of emotions racing through me and how a dead woman landed in front of our door.

Nothing seemed amiss, nothing to indicate how she'd died or where in the heck she might have come from.

"I don't care who she is or what she can do. Your little science experiment just let my niece's killer walk," Sloan growled and pointed at me.

"Science experiment?" I said, "if it wasn't for this little science experiment, you'd still be scratching your ass trying to figure out who he is. If it wasn't for this science experiment, you'd have no connection to the killer at all." My voice grew louder with each word until my own anger rivaled that of Sloan's.

Noah stepped between us and held up his hand. "I don't want to shoot either of you, so cool it." Noah nodded toward the hotel. "Walk away, Sloan." Noah turned to me, and I refused to meet his gaze, mine still locked on the recipient of my mood. "Lucy, you're up to bat. Let's go see if we can make your emotional connection stronger to the victim's and try to retrace her steps."

I stomped inside the elevator with Ford and Tines as my escorts. Noah had stayed in the lobby with Sloan.

"Just who in the hell does he think he is?" I crossed my arms over my chest and continued to glare at my own reflection in the elevator door, getting more irritated that we hadn't reached the floor.

"You don't want to piss him off, Lass," Tines said.

Tines never said much, like ever. He was strong and protective and knew his way around weapons, but he was like the silent brooding type.

"And why is that?" I asked.

"Because he's loaded, and when I say loaded, I don't mean in the puissant-billionaire-type loaded. I'm talking he's already bought his condo on the moon and loaded his two rocket ships in his garage ready to go on a moment's notice."

"You think I care about his money?" A laugh exploded from my lips. Only it wasn't funny haha; it was more of a "bite my ass" kind of thing. I liked to think I wasn't a person who could be bought. My parents had raised me to fight for everything I own and to appreciate it more because I earned it. Nothing would be handed to me on a silver platter, and I didn't expect it to.

"Obviously not," Ford answered. "Still, he's not a man to trifle with, Lucy. He's good at getting his way, and if he wants you off this task force, it's as good as done."

"He doesn't scare me. Let him send me back." I tossed my hands up in the air. "Maybe Sloan is smart enough to figure this out on his own."

"You don't get it, Lass" Tines said. "You piss off Sloan, he'll see that you aren't sent back to the psych ward. He'll makes sure the judge knows you're sane enough to be doing jail time. Don't piss him off."

I wasn't making promises. The man called me a science project. Asshat.

16

Lucy didn't have any stake in this game. Had it been her sister that was killed, she wouldn't be screwing around with this guy. She would have already slit his throat. That Lucy was the one Sloan needed. Not this chick that wanted to play games.

Sloan slid up to the hotel bar, laid a twenty on the counter, and ordered a shot of Jack Daniels. Noah and Hunt had promised Sloan results. Was it that damn bracelet that had her acting like an angel?

Sloan tossed the shot back. It burned on the way to his gut as he watched the group of sorority girls at the other end of the bar. Each had on a see-through T-shirt covering their barely-there bathing suits.

"They may be fine, but they've got nothing on that hot redhead you stole from me," a college-aged guy said as he slid up onto the stool next to Sloan.

Sloan turned to look at the guy. It was the same young wet-behind-the-ears college kid that Lucy had been dancing with at the club. "What can I say? I see something I want, I go after it."

"I bet she was a tight little jam, wasn't she?" the guy asked, sliding his empty beer bottle toward the bartender.

"You obviously didn't get to know her very well. What makes you think anything about the redhead was easy?"

"I could have persuaded her." The college kid slid off the bar stool, almost falling on his butt. "I still might, if I ever see her again."

"Good luck with that," Sloan said, ordering another drink as the college kid staggered away.

One of the women at the end of the bar was staring seductively at Sloan. If he wanted, he could get her into bed, without even buying her dinner. But it wasn't the easy young naïve women that he wanted. No, he wanted someone much more headstrong, much more willing to push back and not give in. He could only imagine their fights being like Fourth of July fireworks and their make-up sex being hotter than anything he could even imagine. His body hardened at the thought. Lucy was like a wet dream, and Sloan was having a hard time staying focused on finding his niece's killer. He needed to keep his head in the game if he was going to help Lucy find the killer and avenge his niece. He'd let anger get the best of him when he'd made the science experiment comment. It wasn't anger at her but at Gentry.

Lucy was a combustible force that intrigued Sloan, and he wasn't the only one. Ford had the same hungry look in his eye, and he never managed to piss her off. There was something about Lucy that demanded a man to take notice. Maybe it was those lips that begged to be kissed or the thought of exploring her body...every last inch.

"Eyes on the prize," he muttered, sliding off the stool. He downed the second shot and winked at the college girl across the bar. No reason to destroy her fantasy.

Sloan had made it back up to Lucy's hotel floor where the others were staying. Lucy was sitting in the hallway outside the suite door with her legs crossed, as if she were meditating. Sloan leaned against the wall. Tines was on one end of the hallway, redirecting the hotel guests to take the stairs.

Noah shrugged as if answering his unasked question.

Sloan squatted next to her. "Sorry, princess."

Lucy just tilted her head as if she didn't hear him. Heck, she probably didn't.

Lucy's eyes shot open, and she jumped up from the floor and started at a jog toward where Tines was redirecting. She passed him at a fast clip and headed for the hotel stairs.

Tines took off after her while Noah and Sloan followed behind. They'd just reached the stairs to find she was already two levels down.

"Wait up, Lucy," Noah called out.

"I can't. If I stop, I might lose the connection," she yelled back. Her voice echoed off the concrete steps.

They caught up with her as she was arguing with an employee, trying to gain entrance into a restricted area. Noah flashed his badge, and the employee stepped aside.

She took off at a run again, only this time she slowed as she stepped into the laundry area. Floor-to-ceiling machines lined the space. The heat from the dryers made sweat bead on Sloan's brow, and yet Lucy seemed determined and unyielding to anyone who gave her questionable looks.

Tines was right behind her. She slowed in front of a door that was labeled, Danger: Stay Out.

She touched the handle and closed her eyes. "She came from here."

Lucy yanked the door open when Tines grabbed her arm to stop her from going inside. He pulled her behind him as Noah and Sloan pulled out their guns.

"What's down there?" he asked one of the employees.

"The abandoned laundry and boiler room. No one uses it anymore," the worker answered.

Noah snapped on a light and entered first, and Sloan followed, easing down into the florescent-lit flickering space. A green glow from the bulbs danced in the shadows. The smell was musty, the floors dirty. It wasn't just creepy; it was damn near arrogant if the killer had been keeping her in this room. So close to employees who could help her and yet so far away. Taunting her. How did he stifle her screams? All those questions rolled in Sloan's mind as they checked behind every nook and cranny and moved farther into the belly of the beast.

His breath caught as anger built in his gut. Pictures of Lucy hung on the wall. Pictures of her from the club. Pictures of her from the hotel, from the parking lot, and pictures of her and him kissing. That one had a knife sticking through his head.

"Look at this," Tines called out from around the back of an old dryer.

They stepped around to see Tine's discovery, and

Lucy's hand flew to cover her mouth. There was a wooden X standing in the corner of the room with arm and leg restraints attached. Dried bloodstains saturated several places.

"Is this where he tortures them?" Sloan's voice sounded foreign to his own ears.

"There's no face prosthetics down here. Even if he is keeping them here, this isn't his final destination. The one that got away was lucky. The fact she ended up on our floor wasn't coincidence.

"I bet she has a room in the hotel and Gentry doesn't even know she slipped away." Lucy said.

"That means he'll be back," Sloan said, releasing the magazine clip on his gun and checking the bullets. "And I'll be waiting."

Lucy slammed her hand against the dried blood and shut her eyes. A scream ripped from her lips as she dropped to her knees without releasing her touch.

"It's too dark to see his face, but she's scared for her life."

"Doesn't she normally tap into the killer?" Tines asked Noah.

"In this case, the victim's energy is all she has to work with. The killer was never in our hallway."

Tines nodded.

"Oh God, he stabbed her." Lucy's head fell forward; her hair shielded her face. "Be a good girl while we play and I may let you live." Lucy shook her head as if it were her answering the maniac. "She can't see his face."

Several minutes ticked by before Lucy dropped her

hand and opened her eyes. "The son of a bitch raped her."

"Tell me you saw his face, heard his voice. Tell me you've got something to nail this son of a bitch," Noah growled.

Lucy stumbled to her feet like a drunk sailor. Her eyes started to roll in her head, and Sloan grabbed her before she fell. "The woman's fear drained me. I need some air."

Sloan lifted her in his arms. "I'll take her by the pool while you call in the forensic team."

"Sloan," Noah called out. "Don't let her out of your sight. This maniac knows she's been staying in this building. That's why he picked this place. He's been watching her."

"I've got her."

17

I awoke on a cushioned beach chair inside a bungalow on the hotel patio. The ocean breeze caressed my face. The fear I'd experienced through witnessing the college girl's captivity had stolen every bit of energy in my body. It could've been worse. Instead of fear, it *could* have been the killer's rage still coursing through my body. The need and desire to kill was something much harder to shake.

Sloan sat on the lawn chair across from me. The pool was practically empty, as dark clouds hovered above. Sloan was a hard man to figure out. The intensity swirled in his deep blue eyes, calling to me, but also frightening me. It was an unexplainable emotion.

"Welcome back," he said.

"Hunting like that always leaves me vulnerable." A shuddered ran up my spine even uttering the word. Vulnerable wasn't an adjective that was used to describe me. "Intense emotions drain me. There was one case before where I couldn't get out of bed for two whole days."

"Was that when you were tracking Carl?"

"Not Carl. Another dirt-bag serial killer. One the Department still hasn't caught."

"You think they're related?"

I shook my head. "Not possible."

"Why is that?" he asked.

"That killer targets men and his emotions were all over the place."

"And you keep all of these connections in your head?"

"Until either I die or they die." I tossed my legs over the side of the chair and tried to stand, realizing too late that I was still too woozy.

Sloan rose as fast as I did and tried to ease me back down onto the chair. "How do you get your strength back?"

"It dehydrates me. I don't know if it has to do with the serum that they used in the trials or what, but a bottle of water would do wonders for me."

Sloan glanced from me toward the bar just inside the patio doors.

"I promise not to move."

He looked resigned. "See that you don't."

I saluted him as if he were one of my babysitters. Truth was I still knew nothing about Sloan, well, nothing other than the way he strummed my body to life and aggravated me just as quickly.

He'd been gone two seconds when the college kid I'd been dancing with stepped into my bungalow with two of his buddies.

"There you are," he said.

I tried to sit up, but the college kid sat down on my chair. "No need to get up. I think we'll keep you on your back. Cover her mouth, boys."

Fear crept my spine as I tried to scream, but the hand covering my mouth blocked any sound. One guy grabbed my arms while the college kid ripped my shirt, exposing my bra. "You almost screwed a guy on the dance floor. This tent should be private enough for you."

I leaned forward bit the hand covering my mouth until his hold loosened and I knocked my skull against the pervert's.

"You bitch," he growled as I squirmed off the chair.

Their buddy was still blocking my exit. "Your turn."

The guy from the dance floor grabbed me around the waist as the exit blocker approached. His fist landed on my jaw. Blood exploded in my mouth as I fought through the pain. My busted lip burned as I spat.

My eyes narrowed as he approached me again. This time I saw him coming and kicked with the force of an NFL kicker, hitting him in his jewels. He went down on a howl as I head-butted the guy from the dance floor behind me.

His hold loosened, and that was all the wiggle room I needed. I stumbled from the tent and screamed, my legs uncooperative. I slipped on the tile and landed on my hands and knees, my scream getting louder with my need to get away.

The guys took off, disappearing into the shrubbery. I inhaled a calming breath, and that was when I spotted him. Gentry, on the other side of the pool. The shadows did little to conceal his identity.

"What the hell happened?" Sloan asked, dropping the water bottle. He gathered me in his arms and plopped down on one of the pool chairs.

"The guy from the club and his buddies attacked me."

Sloan's gaze narrowed. "He did this?"

I swallowed hard and pointed toward the shadows. "And Gentry was across the pool. I saw him."

Sloan pulled out his phone and sent a text before lifting me into his arms and carried me inside the hotel, into the elevator. He didn't let me down until he had me inside the hotel room.

"What the hell did you do to her?" Ford asked as he and Sam walked back into the hotel room returning from the crime scene in the laundry room.

"He didn't do this. The kid from the club attacked me with his buddies."

Ford pegged Sloan with his glare. "And where were you?"

"Don't blame Sloan. I sent him to get me water, and the college kids found me vulnerable. It's my own fault."

Sam stood in the doorway to my room with his arms crossed. "You say it was the kid from the bar?"

"Yeah, it was him all right."

Sam handed me a wet washcloth, and a hiss escaped my mouth as I dabbed at my busted lip. I probably had more scratches and bruises that they couldn't see, but I didn't like them seeing me like this, weak and needy.

Sloan's jaw tightened. "We need to take you to the hospital so we have proof of what happened. We'll press charges and get him arrested. They'll be lucky if the cops get to them before I do."

"I'm fine; I don't need the hospital. I got away before he could do anything."

Sam's gaze landed on my busted lip. "I'll eviscerate him online. I'm going to hack every single one of his accounts and take away anything and everything that he loves."

I've never had anyone willing to go to bat for me other than my sister. Sam's determination made my heart squeeze. "How are you going to do that if you don't have a clue who he is?"

"Are you kidding?" Sam asked. "I identified him the minute you dragged him to the dance floor."

"And while Sam attacks him on the computer, don't you worry, Lucy. I'll be taking everything else he's got," Ford said.

A man willing to steal for me. Another one willing to destroy online. I never thought I'd meet guys who cared as much other than my brother-in-law. Maybe there was something to having friends to watch my back.

"I can take care of this when our case is over. I don't want you guys getting into any trouble."

"Trouble is my middle name," Sam said. "Besides no one screws with my new friends. Don't worry, Lucy Loo. With a few keystrokes he'll never know what hit him."

"Besides destroying the college kid, do you know what would help me more?" I asked.

"Name it," Sam said.

"Gentry was in the building. He was by the pool." I explained.

"And you're telling us this now?" Sam asked.

"I texted Noah before I brought Lucy upstairs." Sloan answered.

"Can you pull up surveillance to see what he was up to?" I asked.

Ford spent the next twenty minutes taking pictures of my cuts and bruises as evidence of the assault.

With each click, anger stirred in my gut. Anger with the pricks who did this and anger with myself for almost letting it happen.

I grabbed a first aid kit and some towels and stepped into the bathroom. Sloan followed me, and I held out my hand to stop him. "You and I have chemistry. You entering the bathroom isn't what I need right now. I need to get cleaned up. I need to tend to my wounds, and if you were to stay in here with me, none of that would get done."

The adjoining bathroom door opened, and Ford was staring at us. "I thought you might need help. It seems Sloan and I had the same idea."

"I can handle this myself. I need to take a shower, alone." I glanced to each of them before leaning into the shower and turning on the faucet to get the hot water running.

Sloan waited for Ford to shut the door, and then his heated gaze landed on mine. "You sure you don't need help?"

"I'm fine." I planted my hand on his chest, backing him out the door. I slowly closed it in his face.

Tears gathered in my eyes as I stared at my face in the mirror. My busted lip, the bags beneath my eyes, the bruises on my cheek starting to turn an ugly mixture of blue and purple. It wasn't the physical violence that had me struggling to breathe. It was the thought of them actually succeeding in what they'd tried to do. Anger stirred in my belly as the heat from the shower fogged the mirrors.

Fear cramped my gut and I gasped to find words written on the mirror that were uncovered by the steam. *I see you, Lucy.*

I heaved while tightening my fist. I threw the door open and ran out into the living room. "He's been in here."

Sam glanced up at me. "Who?"

"Gentry, he left me a message on the bathroom mirror."

"How in the hell did he do that?" Ford said as each of them took off into the bathroom.

I had no idea how he'd gotten into the room; I only know that he had. I stepped back into my bedroom, looking for anything and everything that might be out of place.

I opened the drawer; all of my panties and bras were gone.

I hurried to the closet and swung it open. All of the clothes that I'd hung up were gone too, and in their place was nothing but red dresses.

I didn't know which one of the guys called Noah and Tines. Heck, I didn't even remember them entering the suite. I sat on the balcony. Sloan had handed me a glass of wine, as if the alcohol would make me relax. The glass remained full in my grasp as I stared out at the waves, thinking that my emotions and life were just as tumultuous as the waves crashing the shore. Little by little they were eating away the shoreline and drawing the sand and mud back into the water. Erosion, that explained me.

Sam had pulled up all the surveillance from all around the hotel and determined that housekeeping was the only person in the room while we were all out. Only our housekeeper was a guy who knew how to avoid the cameras. Gentry had spent twenty minutes in our room with no one to watch him. In twenty minutes, he could have done a ton more damage than just written on the mirror and replaced my clothes.

Tines stepped out onto the balcony with the phone in his hand. "Lass, the phone is for you."

"Who is it?"

"Grant."

I snatched the phone from his hand and covered the speaker. "Did you tell him?"

"He has a right to know."

"If he leaves my sister vulnerable and comes here, I'm blaming you."

Tines' eyes softened. "You're his family too. If he wants to be here to protect you, you should respect that. "

My eyes narrowed at Tines. "You don't want me on your bad side, teddy bear."

Tines laughed as he headed back into the suite.

I took a calming breath and placed the phone next to my ear. "I don't know what they told you, but I'm fine. I put more of a hurting on those college kids than they put on me."

"What college kids, Lucy?" Grant asked.

Crap. I was sure that Tines had told him what happened. "Just some punks. It's nothing to worry about."

"Nothing to worry about, like the fact that Gentry had access to your room?"

"I wasn't in it."

"Lucy, I'll be on the first flight out."

"No, you won't. If you leave Gigi, I'm going to be pissed and back out of finding this monster. I swear to God. I don't even care if they put me in jail."

"Dammit, Lucy, if anything happens to you, she's going to blame me."

"And if anything happens to her, I'm going to blame

you. Which one of us would you rather have mad at you?"

I hadn't wanted to dream of serial killers or college guys, or even Ford or Sloan. I didn't want to dream of anything, but I did. I dreamt of a time with my sister when we were younger on a playground. It was a sweet dream until it wasn't. Until I spotted the college kid and Gentry off in the distance, talking to each other and pointing at Gigi and me. Darkness filled their eyes when their laughing stopped, and they stomped in our direction.

My eyes flew open as I struggled to calm my racing heart. I stared at the ceiling fan as it went round and round and round. The sheet clung like a second skin to my dampened body, but at least I didn't scream. I turned toward the alarm clock. The red numbers glowed 6 AM. Memories of the night before flashed in my mind as the bruise on my lip started to throb. Everything was coming back to me now. I was hunting a killer, and I'd almost become a victim. I slid out of the bed and stepped into the shower. The hot water sliced down my body, waking up my pores and my brain. I got out. The words on the mirror were no longer readable. One of the guys must have removed them. While I dressed, I heard two voices coming from the direction of the living room. I opened the door and stepped out. The chill on the cold tile had me heading straight toward the coffee pot. I was going to need a ton of caffeine, especially today.

Sloan and Ford were giving each other the stink eye.

Sam was behind his keyboard, typing away, his knee jumping and tapping his foot at each keystroke. Noah was casually dressed in jeans and a pullover shirt. His badge clung to his hip.

"Morning, guys what's on the agenda today?"

"I ordered surveillance on Gentry this morning," Noah said.

"I pulled his and his father's financials to find out how many areas in town he actually owns and can be hiding out," Sam said from across the room without even a pause in his typing. "He has five properties, three houses, a boat in a slip at the marina, and a bar on the strip."

"We don't have any physical evidence to tie Gentry to the killings, yet. So that should be our objective today."

A knock on the door stopped all conversation.

"Are you expecting company?" I asked Noah as I headed toward the door.

Sloan stepped in my way, stopping me. "I'll get it. For all we know Gentry is standing out on the landing with a gun."

Although it was possible, Gentry wasn't stupid enough to do that. Sloan opened the door to find a college kid dressed in hotel garb standing on the other side. He had an envelope in his hand. "Is this where Lucy is staying?"

"Who wants to know?" Noah asked as he approached the door.

The kid lifted the envelope in the air. "Somebody left this at the bar, and it has her name and room number on it."

Noah slid a pair of gloves out of his pocket and

snapped them on. The college kid looked on confused as Noah took the envelope and walked back into the room.

Sloan tipped the kid some cash and shut the door on his face. Noah took out his pocket knife and slid it under the tab, trying not to disturb any DNA. He pulled out a note and held it up by the corner.

"What does it say?" I asked.

"Happy birthday?" Noah answered.

I had completely forgotten it was my birthday. My days had started to run together. "Is that all?"

Noah put the letter on the counter and rushed to the balcony door. He pulled it open and stepped out.

I followed him and his gaze down below. My breath hitched. "Is that what I think it is?"

Noah left me standing on the balcony as he grabbed his phone and headed out the suite door. Before he closed it, he pointed at Sloan. "You stay here with her. No one in or out of the door." He slammed the door behind him as he left.

Three dead bodies were floating face down in the pool, which was filled with their blood. I recognized the clothes. The young men from last night. "Those are the guys who attacked me."

"Looks like somebody did us a favor," Sloan said as Ford and Sam stepped out onto the balcony.

"If Lucy hadn't been on lockdown, I might've thought it was her," Ford said.

"If I hadn't been on lockdown, I would have most definitely been responsible," I said.

I should have felt bad that they died, that they were targeted because of me. Yet I felt nothing, no emotion one way or the other. Maybe it was the acknowledgment of knowing that they wouldn't attack me again, or maybe I was just in a state of shock. Either way, I felt nothing. I stepped back into the suite and left the others on the balcony. I walked over to the counter where Noah had dropped the letter.

Happy Birthday.
I left your present in the pool. They made a mistake by touching what is mine.

19

Gentry was winning in the brains department. I had a room full of muscle that was waiting on me to produce some viable information. He may have done me a favor by removing my would-be rapist from the face of the earth, but that didn't mean that I had changed my mind about seeing Gentry six feet under.

I was tired of his games, tired of being two steps behind. I was tired of him knowing what we were going to do before we did it. It was time I changed from being the stalked to the stalker, the whole reason I was in this tourist town. Find him, and destroy him, before he could kill me.

I didn't need peace for what I was about to do; I needed Gentry angry. I needed something to tap into, to find him, like a fish on the line. I needed him to take the bait so I could reel him in. I dumped my coffee down the sink and grab three bottles of water out of the fridge, downing my first one. I knew I wasn't supposed to leave the hotel by myself, but I could almost guarantee the others wouldn't agree with what I was about to do.

I stepped into my room and changed into the red dress that I'd worn that night at the club. I slipped out of the suite. Only Sam saw me. I held my finger to my lips and mouthed that I'd be right back.

He nodded and pointed to his wrist to remind me that I was being monitored, probably by him.

I held up five fingers. I didn't expect to be gone long, just long enough. I took the stairs down to the lobby and stepped out the front doors. Just as I'd expected, news vans started to arrive. As each person entered, I opened my senses to gauge their determination until I found a female reporter whose persistence registered off the charts.

I stepped in her way. "Excuse me. This is your lucky day."

Her gaze slid down my dress, and she rolled her eyes. "This isn't your chance for five seconds of fame; we have a real crime to report."

"Five bodies scattered around the beach area, a serial killer in our midst, and I'm the connection. Now you can either go report on the three dead college kids in the pool, who died after trying to rape me last night, or you can hear me out and get the inside scoop before your rivals."

She exchanged a look with the cameraman. "There were only five dead girls."

"Six, the last one was found yesterday in this very hotel."

"What's your angle? What do you want?"

"I need your help. I need to get my message out. I just need you to promise me that, no matter what or who tries to stop you from airing it, you try everything in your power to get my message on air."

She nodded, and I took her by the arm and led her over toward the trees, out of view of the lobby. Taking a deep breath, I stared at the red light as the cameraman began to record.

"Let's start by telling us your name."

"I'm Dr. Lucy Bray, the person who captured serial killer Carl Chisolm and almost killed him."

The reporter shared a look with the cameraman again. "What can you tell me about the recent string of deaths on the beach?"

"They aren't over." I shrugged. "Most of the girls were taken because they looked like me and were wearing a red dress. The killer isn't picky, but he's smart. Of course, not smarter than me." I winked at the camera lens. "Are you?"

"Do you know who this killer is?" she asked.

I tilted my head with a cocky smile. "A low-life man from my past, who didn't even stand out enough for me to remember his name. He wants what he can't have, and his daddy's money can't buy me. He's getting sloppier with each kill. His last victim escaped her bindings and was almost home free." I stared directly into the camera. "I'm coming for you. I am going to stop you, and when I do, you won't have an attorney to hide behind."

"Lucy," Noah growled, and the camera spun in his direction.

The reporter glanced at Noah's badge. "Special

Agent, do you have an ID on this killer, and can you confirm that there are six women now dead instead of five?"

Noah's eye twitched as he took me by the arm. "We don't comment on active investigations."

"But, sir," the reporter called out, following us to the elevator. "She hasn't told me who the dead guys are in the pool."

"No comment," he said as the doors slid closed.

"Have you lost your damn mind?" Noah growled, pegging me with his glare.

"I needed to make him angry to try and connect to him again. Don't worry; I made myself a target."

Noah grabbed me by the arm and pulled me out of the elevator, shoving me inside the suite. "When we get back, you'll be lucky if you don't get jail time instead of the psych ward. Now you stay here while I go confiscate that interview."

"You can't," I said, trying to block the door.

Noah glanced over his shoulder at Tines. "You're in charge. Medicate her if need be."

My mouth parted as Tines eased me out of the way. I tossed my hands up in the air, defeated.

"I wouldn't worry about it, Lucy. He's not going to reach the news crew in time," Sam said, gesturing to the TV with the remote in his hand. He turned on the volume just in time for my voice to cascade through the speakers.

"They did it," I whispered.

"Congratulations, you called the killer an idiot and made yourself a target."

"I know." I couldn't hide the excitement strumming through my body. "Now I just hope he sees this."

"Looks like he caught the live clip," Sam said, pausing the TV. He pointed to onlookers in the background. "Isn't that your boy?"

Seeing Gentry standing by, watching me, was even better than I could have hoped for. Now I just needed him to act on it.

I grabbed some water bottles, went to my room, and climbed up on my bed. Crossing my legs as if I was going to meditate, I closed my eyes, searching and waiting for that tug of anger brewing beneath Gentry's surface waiting to spill free. If I was lucky, I wouldn't have to wait long.

20

SLOAN

It took Roth an hour to return to the room. His face was red and blotchy, and his entire presence had changed. The once laid-back man who seemed to just be taking everything in stride was irate.

Lucy was a button-pusher. She could take the well-mannered agent and turn him into a raging lunatic; she had skill.

"Where is she?" Noah asked.

"She's in her room, doing that meditating thing where she tries to connect," Ford announced.

"She better hope that she finds something fast. Hunt is on his way, and he's going to want her head on the chopping block," Noah said.

"I'd hate to be her," Ford said.

"He's not going to hurt her, is he?" Sam asked. The little IT guy had developed some type of fascination with the doctor.

"If he doesn't like what she has to say, he's going to

throw her butt in federal prison, not the sissy place where she's been living."

Not if Sloan could help it. This woman was the only connection they had to the killer. It didn't hurt that he liked her. If the killer hadn't killed the ones who tried to rape her, Sloan would have done it himself. No way was he giving her up yet, not until he had what he came for. Sloan pulled out his phone and dialed a number as he stepped out onto the balcony, shutting the door behind him. From inside the room, Noah held his gaze, as if he knew exactly what Sloan was up to.

"Deputy Director Shaw, this is Jack Sloan." His words came out swift and to the point. Neither the head of the FBI or Sloan liked to shoot the breeze. Truth was Melanie Shaw owed him, for more than one thing.

"Jack, I had a feeling you'd be calling me." Shaw chuckled.

"I need a favor," Sloan said.

"I'm sure you do. It doesn't have anything to do with a doctor now, does it? Because I have to tell you, Sloan, it's not pretty where she's going."

"Deputy Director, I need you to loosen your grip on her so she can work."

"Ha," she blurted out. "If anything, we're tightening our grip after the stunt she just pulled. Hunt is already on his way to deliver the ass-chewing."

Sloan lowered his head. "She may not be playing by the rules, but she's close to flushing him out. I can feel it in my gut, Shaw."

"The infamous Sloan gut." She harrumphed.

"That gut saved you more times than I can count. I need her, and I'm calling in one of my favors."

That got Shaw's attention. "She's that important?"

"Would I be calling otherwise?"

"She broke some important laws, Sloan."

"Isn't that why they chose her for the team? Because she can get the job done when others can't?"

"Hunt isn't going to like this," Shaw said.

"Hunt will get over it, if we deliver him this killer on a silver platter. I believe Lucy can deliver him. She just needs room to stretch."

"Are you sure that there isn't more between you and her and that's the reason that you want her around?"

"Shaw, you know me better than that. Catching my niece's killer comes first, and then we can talk about having Lucy released from the psych ward."

"How did I know you were going to say that? Sorry, Sloan, I won't be able to help you there. Hunt has dibs on her. He pulled some strings to make it happen."

"Keep the muzzle on your dog, Shaw. I need this woman; we all need this woman. She's the only connection to this killer. He's fixated on her, and she can draw him out."

"You've got thirty-six hours, and then she's Hunt's to deal with."

"Thanks, Shaw."

"Uh-huh." The line disconnected.

Three hours later, Sam was at the computer typing away, Tines was cleaning his gun, and Noah was staring down at a map of Panama City and the beach where he had certain sites circled. Sites that were believed to be connected to either the killing of these women and/or Gentry.

Sloan rested against the doorjamb, staring into Lucy's room. She'd been sitting in the same position for hours without food or drink. The only thing that was changing was her facial expression.

Noah appeared by Sloan's side. "Has she said anything yet?"

"Not a word," Sloan answered in a whisper. Lucy was running out of time before Hunt showed up and she'd be dragged back to whatever hole they'd pulled her out of. They all needed something. Even if she couldn't connect to the killer anymore, at least they knew who it was, who they were dealing with. "What proof do we have Gentry is the killer?"

"The biker watching us at the scene and him following Lucy. You have to admit that he's fixated on her."

"We need more." Sloan said.

"We started surveillance on Gentry and every place he's either dumped bodies and on the properties tied to him or his father."

"Noah, you should come take a look at this."

Before either of them could move, Lucy's eyes flew open. Fear and anger stared back at them.

"He's hunting for a new girl."

"Any idea where he is?" Noah asked.

"Yeah, the first club where we tried to find him. I

recognized it." Lucy slid off the bed in a hurry and ran out of the bedroom to grab her shoes.

Tines and Ford watched in curiosity.

"How can you be so sure it's the same place?" Ford asked.

Lucy rolled her eyes. "There's no time to explain."

"Make time," Noah answered.

Lucy sighed. "You know how I work. I tap into emotions; it's how I connect. I tap into the emotions from the crime scene. Each person gives off a different vibration. Gentry's anger, or any other exorbitant emotion, sets off the vibration that I can cling to and follow. The last several hours, I've been waiting for him."

"To get angry?" Sloan asked.

"To make a mistake and he did." Lucy walked back into the room and grabbed the bottles of water, downing one before she came up for air. "You know how we never realized how Gentry knew me? Well I might have just figured it out."

Lucy walked over to Sam and leaned over his computer table. "Gentry just gave himself a shot. The insignia on the vial was the same as the one from the government trial I was in, the Mind Stalker program. The way he knows me must be from that group."

"Like Carl?" Noah asked.

"Just like Carl. I wouldn't be surprised if they were partners."

"Serial killers tend to work alone," Noah said. "And it doesn't make sense. Gentry comes from a wealthy family, and Carl was working as a mailman and a menial job in your program."

"Gentry's daddy is a millionaire. Maybe Gentry was looking for something that money can't buy. Maybe he was Carl's protégé. It would explain how he became either fixated on Gigi or, if he was in the program, how he became fixated on me. Regardless, that shot he just took wasn't like mine. It was the opposite. Where mine calms me down to put me to sleep, Gentry's did the opposite for him. It enhanced his anger to the point that he's ready to kill anybody in his way."

"We need to send his picture to Grant to start digging around in the governmental program's database of participants and employees. It shouldn't be hard to associate Gentry if he was involved."

"You can chase that rabbit later. Right now, Gentry is ready to kill and I bet he'll strike again soon. Bar Wars is scheduled again for tonight."

"And you got all of that just by meditating?" Tines asked.

"I knew he'd mess up," I answered.

"How do you know this isn't a trap?" Sloan asked as crossed his arms over his chest. Gentry was smarter than their average criminal. His desire was what drove him. He'd yet to make a mistake that they could catch, and this had the word trap written all over it.

"Do you want to take the chance that he gets another girl? What if she ends up like your niece and you could have been the one to stop him?"

"I don't like it," Sloan said.

"Then stay here. Let me go. That's why they brought me. Use me as the diversion, as bait. Bait that he won't be able to deny. Hell, let him get his hands on me." Lucy lifted her arm and shook the bracelet on it. "You know how to track me. You'll save me because you have to. I won't let him take another girl."

"I haven't agreed to let you go anywhere, much less with us when we go after him," Noah said.

"Lucy has a point," Tines said. "It's always better to be on the offensive than the defensive. Up until now we've been chasing him, not knowing his next move. If Lucy thinks she can predict that, and we can track her, it's our best move."

"I don't like that idea," Sam said from across the room. "This guy has been killing women like her. What makes you think that he's even going to take her back to his little hideout to do the deed? What if he kills her in a back alley somewhere? You might not have time to get to her."

Lucy crossed the room and kissed Sam's cheek. "Your worry is sweet, no matter how unfounded. Don't forget what I did to Carl. I can take care of myself."

This argument was going nowhere fast. Tines and Lucy were ready to head out the door. Sloan could tell just by the reaction on Noah's face that he was debating on letting them go. Apprehension settled in Sloan's gut. They were playing right into Gentry's hand.

"He knows you can tap into his anger. He knows you'll try to save the girl. He knows that you'll come after him. How is any of that supposed to be a surprise? Hell, you even told him about the tracker in your bracelet."

Aggravation settled on Lucy's face. "What do you suggest, hotshot?"

"I suggest you be smart. The only reason you had the

upper hand on Carl was because he didn't see you coming. Gentry can see you coming."

"How do you suggest we take back the element of surprise?" Lucy asked.

"That's simple. You don't go," Sloan said. "He's going to be looking for you. He's going to be angry that you aren't there. Tap into that anger and pinpoint his location. Let us do the rest."

Lucy's mouth snapped open and then closed again. "I'm the one who can find him."

"That's what these are for," Sloan said, picking up the ear microphones. "You get us in the general vicinity, and we'll find him. You already told us he was at a club. Let us be the ones to flush him out."

21

Fifteen minutes later, only Sam and I remained in the room while the others loaded up for the hunt. I knew they had a point. I didn't have to be there in order to take him out. I just wanted to be.

Sam was sitting at his computer, his fingers tapping across the keyboard as if he was in his own zone. "Lucy, I hacked the security feed for the club. My facial recognition program hasn't spotted him yet."

I didn't know why I was so apprehensive. Maybe it was the fact that I wasn't watching things with my own eyes and had to rely on others to give me the information. Sloan had been right. Carl had been caught off guard, Gentry wouldn't be. At least not yet. When I didn't show up for his capture, he was going to get pissed. The only thing that wasn't making sense was the fact I wasn't feeling his unease. I wasn't feeling his anger. I wasn't even feeling his excitement. It was like he'd cut off all of his emotion strings to stop me from being able to track his movements. His participation in the Mind Stalker program made sense now. The way he knew to block her. The moment I opened my eyes on my bed, I gotten my first taste of his anger.

"Lucy, why don't you sit down," Sam said from across the room.

As if that were possible. I stepped into the kitchen and started opening drawers. This might be the only opportunity I had to find what I needed.

"Are you hungry? I could cook you something," Sam said.

I held out my wrist. "I'm not hungry. I'm looking for something to jam into little slide so I can open the bracelet. There aren't tiny sharp objects in this room." I raise my brow as I stared at him. "You happen to have a needle in a sewing kit? Maybe something similar?"

"Noah would kill me if I helped you get out of that bracelet. Besides, it's not a good idea considering everything going on. We need to be able to keep eyes on you more than any of the others."

I tossed the knife back into the silverware drawer and slammed it shut. Just because they thought they needed to keep eyes on me didn't mean that I wanted them to. I continued searching the kitchen, and Sam started typing on the computer again; my attempts at freedom were no longer his concern.

I walked through the suite and tossed open the door to Ford's room. His was an exact replica of mine. My gaze traveled over the room to his suitcase then to the suits hanging up in the closet. Ford was a thief. He had to have some type of lock picks to help me.

I opened his dresser drawer and rummaged around

inside trying to put everything back as I found it. I slammed it closed and worked my way through the rest of them.

I turned around again, gazing over the room. If I were a thief wanting to hide my tools, where would I hide them? My gaze went up to the vents in the ceiling. No, he wasn't tall enough to reach them. Slowly, again, I gazed around the room, and my eyes landed on his closet. I ran my hands through all of his suit pockets, hoping beyond anything that maybe he had stashed something useful in there. I hit pay dirt on a dark blue suit jacket that matched his eyes. There was a hidden pocket inside. I could feel the outline of something beneath the fabric. I just couldn't make out what it was. I grabbed the suit jacket out of the closet and tossed it onto the bed.

It only took a few attempts to open the hiding spot. A missing stitch in the seam, clever. I reached inside and pulled out a leather case and opened it. "Jackpot."

"Lucy, I don't think Ford would appreciate you being in his room and going through his things," Sam said from the doorway.

"Well, the safety pin I normally use to get out of my restraints is in a trashcan at the airport. I had to ditch it to go through the metal detector."

"Lucy, if Noah finds out about this, he's going to send you back. You won't be able to help us catch Gentry."

Sam had a point. I knew it, and he knew it. Whatever choice I was about to make would define my future. My gaze shifted to the lock pick set sitting open on the bed. The one I needed was nestled inside. I could take it and remove my restraints and run. I could be free.

"Lucy, come in." Noah's voice traveled into the earpiece in my ear.

Sam reached over, grabbed my hand, and pushed the button on the earpiece, showing me how it worked. "I'm here."

"What are you feeling, anything? Is he angry? Does he already have her? We haven't been able to spot him in the crowd."

I closed my eyes and held a deep breath, searching for the tendril of energy and emotion that would take me to him. I felt nothing. "He's not feeling anything. I can't find him yet."

The lights in the room flickered out, making my heart seize. "The lights are out."

Within another second, the fire alarm blared throughout the building. Sam gave me a worried look.

"Noah, the fire alarm is going off, and the lights are out." My voice held a touch of uncertainty.

"That could be him trying to flush you out," Noah said.

"Or it could just be college kids playing a prank," Sam said.

"Or the building could really be on fire," I interjected.

"What do you want us to do?" Sam asked.

"Evacuate the building with the other guests. Don't go wandering off. Stay in the crowd," Sloan ordered. "We're on our way back."

Sloan wasn't the boss of us. "Agent Roth?"

"You heard the man. Do not leave the property. Stay with the other people. Don't make yourself a target," Noah added.

Every nerve in my body told me that Gentry was behind this, regardless of whether or not I could latch onto his emotions. I left the lock pick set on the bed as Sam ushered me out of the hotel room, locking the door behind him.

22

My heart raced as Sam and I headed for the fire exit stairwell. I didn't see any black or gray smoke billowing in the air, but I could smell it. "I'm sure it's nothing, probably just some college kid smoking in his room who passed out and forgot to put out his cigarette."

I didn't know why I expected Sam to believe me when I didn't buy it myself. I didn't believe in coincidences. We shoved out into the parking lot with all the other guests slowly taking their time to get out of the building. They must've been thinking the same thing. I still didn't see the smoke, or even know where it might be coming from, until one of the other guests pointed out there was smoke near the pool area.

"Well, we were wrong; it wasn't a false alarm."

An unease settled firmly in my gut as I glanced around the crowd of people. Gentry's face wasn't among them. When the fire truck pulled into the parking lot, the crowd had to disperse. It wasn't until the alarm was turned off and people were allowed back into their rooms that Sam and I stepped onto the elevator. A hand flew out to stop the door from closing.

Gentry's smiling face stared back at us, and my heart stopped. I'd been right. The barrel of a gun was held to Sam's head. "I know you don't care what happens to you, Lucy. But do you care about what happens to him?"

Gentry used his other hand to jab the number to the service floor where the laundry was located. I inhaled a deep breath of his anger, letting it soak into me. If there was any chance of us getting out of this, I might need to look at Gentry as if he were part of Carl's transgressions.

The door swished open, and the laundry floor was empty of employees. Gentry ushered us through the room with the barrel of the gun at Sam's back. He stopped at the boiler room door. Anger riddled his face.

"Open it."

I swallowed hard, knowing that this might be the place where we both died. "You know, Gentry, even though I called you stupid earlier, you didn't have to prove me right."

"Shut up and get inside." He shoved me forward and I stumbled down the stairs and caught myself on the railing. "Keep moving." Gentry cocked the trigger with the barrel pressed to Sam's head to get him to move. He shut the door behind him and flicked a lock before guiding Sam down the steps.

The light illuminated above us. "Don't worry, Lucy. This isn't where you're going to die."

I gasped as Gentry lifted the gun and hit Sam over the

back of the head. Sam collapsed onto the concrete floor, and I dropped to my knees.

"I'll deal with him later. You're the one I want. Get on your feet," Gentry growled.

"Before you kill me, answer one thing. Why are you changing the women to look like me?"

Gentry neared and pulled a needle out of his pocket. He flicked the cap off, and I scrambled to my feet and began to back away.

"Don't make this difficult," he said, shooting a bullet into the ground near my feet. "Next one is in your head."

He pressed the hard barrel to my skull before shoving the needle into my neck. "You want to know why they look like you?" His voice was stone cold, lacking any emotional inflection. "Don't worry, Lucy. I'll show you exactly why, but first we have to get rid of your tracker. I'd hate for us to be interrupted."

Fear fought the fog forming in my head. If he got rid of the tracker, there would be no one coming to save me. Unable to hold my body up anymore, my eyes rolled in my head, and I dropped to my knees.

Gentry approached with a sharp-looking file in his hand. "Don't fight it, Lucy. We'll be out of here in no time."

Gentry grabbed my hand with the bracelet as I started to lower to the ground, my eyes glazed as I fought to keep them open. Darkness sucked me into its hold.

23

My eyes slowly slid open, taking in the dark room. I yanked at the bindings on my arms and legs. Glancing around the room, I saw I was attached to the same X-shaped board found in the laundry room. Only I wasn't in the same room.

I glanced at my wrist to find the bracelet gone. "Just because you ditch the bracelet doesn't mean they won't find you," I screamed.

"Nice of you to join the land of the living again, not for long but long enough." Gentry chuckled from somewhere behind me.

"If you're going to kill me, just tell me why."

"You don't get to make demands," Gentry said as he stepped around into my view. "Didn't you imply that I was brainless?"

I couldn't answer him. My mouth refused to move as I stared at Gentry. The wig on his head resembled my haircut. Contacts changed his eyes to my color. The prosthetics framing his face to look like mine were flawless. If this guy wasn't such a psycho, he could've easily landed a job in LA working for the movies creating stunt doubles. The clothes he had on were the ones I was just wearing an hour ago. My body was covered in a single T-shirt that came down mid-thigh. Even my bra had been removed.

"You weren't stalking me because you wanted me. You were stalking me because you wanted to *be* me."

Gentry grinned. "And you called me stupid. It took you this long to figure that out."

"Those other girls that you are dressing like me and making to look like me were just prototypes. You were trying to get everything perfect."

Gentry glanced down at my clothes covering his body. "Actually, I think I'm a better you than you were."

He stepped closer to me; his breath laced with liquor. Had that been how he'd blocked his emotions?

"I wouldn't have put Carl in a coma. I would've finished him off."

I was going to die in this room. This guy was crazy. And not in a way that I could stop him, not with my arms and legs bound. I was at his mercy. "We could do it together. What if I helped you? What if I train you?"

"I've watched you enough to know that I could pass as you."

"So, you've been to med school?" I asked.

Gentry's eyes narrowed.

"If you're going to be me, you have to be all me, not just some half-assed version in your head. Unless, of course, you don't have the stones to see this through."

Gentry's nose flared, and anger glinted in his eyes. I

could feel it to my core, soaking in through my pores. "You feel that, don't you? The sweet taste of my anger?"

"Hardly," I answered, trying to piss him off. I needed more; I needed hate to get out of this. I needed to challenge him in a way that he couldn't dismiss, and that would mean cutting me loose even if it was to beat me down.

"How about this?" he asked as he shoved a needle in my neck. "The serum they gave you is useless, but this serum...this will make you a worthy opponent. That's what you want, isn't it? To prove that you're better than me?"

Anger stirred in my veins, turning everything in the room the color red. I yanked at my bindings, letting the restraints cut into my skin just as Gentry used a knife to slice across my chest, mimicking the same wound that I'd given Carl.

"Did you feel that, Lucy?" he sneered. "I promised Carl I would recreate every wound you left on him, and then, when I left you beaten and broken, I'd kill everyone you loved. Starting with your poor little sister, Gigi. She'll be easy. I've already been in her room. I could have killed her many times while she lay helpless in her coma."

I yanked at my bindings again. How did Gentry know my sister was in a coma? That was a question that was going to have to wait. I'd beat it out of him if I have to.

"You think you're better than me?" I spat. "Prove it. Let me down from here and fight me like the bitch I am."

Gentry crossed the room and grabbed another knife from the table. "Now why would I do that? I like you much better where you are."

He slid the knife across my torso, cutting the shirt. A scream flew from my lips. "Wait until I get to the neck. I might have a hard time not stopping."

"God, you can't even do this right. How in the hell do you think you'll pass for me? If you're going to do something right, get it right from the start."

His brows dipped, but his hand with the knife paused.

"I caught him off guard. Carl never saw me coming. I was waiting on him to get home. It was dark when he walked in. He flicked on the light, and when he turned around, I shot him so that he couldn't run off."

Gentry stepped back and picked up his gun. He aimed it at me, and only then did I realize what I'd done. This maniac was going to do the same damage to me.

"Where did you shoot him, Lucy?"

I swallowed hard, trying to think of the best place where I wouldn't lose a lot of blood with him missing and hitting an artery. "His arm."

Gentry tsked and lowered the gun. "Wrong answer."

He lowered the gun to my knee, and I braced myself, unsure I'd be able to handle the pain.

I clenched my eyes closed and cringed, waiting for the inevitable.

The sound of splintered wood had my eyes flying open. The sound of Noah's and Tine's yells made me hang limp against my bindings in relief.

"Get on your knees," Noah growled.

Hesitation filled Gentry's eyes as I started to laugh. "You better do what he says. They don't play around."

Gentry's eyes narrowed.

"Now," Tines added, cocking his trigger. "You have two seconds, or I'll put you on your knees with bullets in your kneecaps."

Gentry dropped the gun and lowered to his knees, and a smile twitched on his lips. "This isn't over, Lucy."

"Yeah, it is," Sloan said, entering the room. He gave one glance at Gentry wearing my dress and shook his head. "The guys in jail are going to love you."

Noah walked over to where I hung; he reached for the bindings. "No, he gave me a shot of something, and I can feel the anger building. Don't untie me until you have my calming shot or some type of restraints to stop me from killing you."

Sloan lifted the needle with my magical elixir and uncapped it. He eased the needle into my arm and pressed the plunger. "Now let's get you down and patched up. We have an ambulance waiting nearby."

"How did you find me?" I asked as Noah undid my restraints. I fell into Sloan's arms.

"I told you that you were being tracked," Noah answered as if I should have known.

"He ditched the bracelet," I said, still unsure where he was going with this.

"The bracelet was a diversion. The minute it was removed, I knew you were either on the run or had been taken. The trackers were added into all of your shoes."

A smile twisted on my lips. "You tricked me."

"Be glad I did," he added as he glanced at Gentry.

At the hospital, Sam burst into the room. His worried gaze settled on me, and relief filled his face. "You're safe."

"I am." I gritted my teeth as the doctor put in the last stitch.

"Good, because we have another problem."

Noah slid his hands into his pockets. "What kind of problem?"

"There's another woman missing."

"What, how do you know?" I asked.

Sam handed the envelope to Noah. "They found this in the boiler room. He was using it as a bargaining chip should he get caught."

"Son of a bitch," I growled as the physician covered my wound. "I didn't see that coming."

"None of us did," Sloan added, stepping into the room.

I sensed the anger thrummed below the surface of his skin. I could feel it across the room. The look on his face was sheer determination and laced with panic.

"That picture is of Susan, my assistant. The woman that was with me at the club. He's got her tied up."

"Well, I guess my job here isn't done." I batted away the physician's fingers and tightened the closure myself. I slid off the bed wearing the scrubs the hospital had given to me. Clothes and shoes that didn't contain any trackers.

"Take me to the jail. He'll talk to me."

"You think he's just going to give up the location?" Sloan asked. "Hell, you couldn't even get him to talk last time."

"Just put me in a room with him for five minutes. I'll get you the location."

"You think beating information out of him is a smart

move, Lucy? He's at the Sheriff's Department. They will arrest you."

"You brought me here so I could get the job done. Now trust me to do it." I headed out of the hospital room with the others following me.

I took a deep breath and clutched the file as I stepped into the room. Gentry didn't look so menacing now. The prosthetics had been ripped from his face, his wig removed. The only remnant was some glue that he'd use to hold it down. His makeup was done like mine. It was a little disorienting to look at him this way. A man that didn't want me but wanted to be me. He was even crazier than I was. I slid into the seat in front of him and watched as he yanked at his bindings.

"I bet this isn't how you expected the day to end."

Gentry gave up on his struggle with the bindings and leaned back in the chair to regard me. I could see it in his eyes; he still thought that he was better than me.

"There is nothing to tie me to those murders that you've investigated. Because I didn't do them. Good luck trying to get a jury to convict me." His voice was smooth and would have been convincing had I not known otherwise.

"I might have believed that, but they have attempted

murder charges for you now...thanks to me." I grinned. "Do you know how giddy that makes me to know that I'm the reason you're going to jail? I guess I really am smarter than you."

"You think I'm going to jail? Take a good look at me, Lucy. How sane do I look? Isn't that the same plea that you took?"

Insanity plea, I should have seen it coming. Any lawyer worth his weight would jump on that bandwagon, and with the type of lawyers that Gentry's father could afford, the trial wouldn't even last a day. I'd read the file on all the places that Gentry had been while in town. Sam had given me a list of the hotels that Gentry had used, and a list of his father's properties. I was positive that Sloan's assistant was in one of those places.

I slipped latex gloves on my fingers keeping a straight face. I slipped opened the file and turned the name for him to see, along with the picture. "You kind of screwed up." I flipped the picture over and pointed to the fingerprint dust that remained. "They've got you, and you did it to yourself."

Gentry visibly swallowed as he lifted his angry gaze to mine. Anger filled the room, and I breathed it in.

"Give me the woman's location, and I'll make sure they don't put you in solitary, because, let me tell you, the woman you took is kind of a big deal to a man with more strings than your daddy."

"What makes you think that I had anything to do with her disappearance?"

"Cut the crap, Gentry. We both know that you are smart enough to kidnap her. We both know how she fits into this puzzle. Tell me where you're hiding her. If she's unharmed, I promise to visit you in prison... Please."

Hearing the word please spew from my lips caught his attention. He leaned back in his chair with a smug look. "You think you're going to be alive to visit me in prison? Carl will be awake soon. He's going to finish what he started. He's going to cut you up as the trash you are, and then he's going do the same thing to your sister. Only with your sister, he's going to feed her dead body to the sharks." Gentry glanced down at the picture, and his lips twitched before he covered it. "And there's not a damn thing you can do about it being locked up in the psych ward."

"Sharks? So that's your play? That's how you know that they'll never find Sloan's assistant." I rose from my seat and slapped the folder closed. I pressed the button in my ear to trigger the earpiece. "Sloan's assistant, Susan, is on Gentry's father's boat. Find the boat, and you'll find her."

I turned to leave and glanced as I grabbed the door-knob. "Thank you for your assistance."

"You stupid bitch. These restraints aren't going to hold me. I'm coming for you; I'm going to make you feel everything that I felt. Your sister is as good as dead. You might as well go ahead and start making her funeral arrangements. Because those are the last arrangements you're ever going to make."

I grinned and closed the door as he yelled more threats.

"How did he do? I asked, handing Sam the folder.

Sam slipped the technology off the back of the folder.

I wouldn't have believed it possible if the others hadn't tried it on me. A device that could indicate deception in a voice if there were enough emotions triggered to find the medium. The entire reason I pissed him off and had offered to visit him in jail. It had set the vocal range to give us enough output.

"You did great. There was no change in his voice when he spoke about the sharks and looked at the picture. He was telling the truth."

I glanced around to find Sloan and Tines gone. "I hope they get her."

"They will," Noah added. "Sam caught him on traffic cams and picked him back up as he neared downtown. Gentry's father owns three properties in that area. You just narrowed it down to a single location."

I pressed my hands together. "Looks like my work is done here. Can I please have a glass of wine now?"

Noah nodded and led the way out of the Sheriff's Department. When we got to the SUV, he answered. "First round of drinks is on me, and if you're lucky, Hunt might even let you stay in the psych ward."

One way or another, I was going to make sure Hunt made good on his promise. Regardless of where I ended up, I'd caught his bad guy, so it was time he paid up on his end of the bargain.

Sloan stayed behind in Florida. They found his assistant, Susan. She was dehydrated and in bad shape.

When our plane landed, my brother-in-law, Grant,

met us at the hangar. I knew something was wrong the minute we stepped off the plane. I didn't know whether it was his look or the rollercoaster of emotions emanating from him, but something was seriously bad.

I closed the distance, dragging my suitcase behind me. "What's wrong?"

"Goddammit," Noah said from behind me as he stared down at his phone.

"Tell me."

"We don't know how he did it, but Gentry escaped."

I calmed the anger in my veins exhaling it before it could settle in my body. It was, a new technique I'd been using to try to battle emotions within. I walked back to Noah and patted his arm. "Don't worry, I know exactly where he's going. It just means I might be delayed getting back to the psych ward."

"Tell me where he's going, and we'll pick him up," Noah demanded.

"You have to trust me this time, Noah. I might not have started out as a team player, but I am now. He's going after my family. I'm positive of it. So, I'll be there when he does. You just have to trust me not to go on the run."

"You've got one week." Noah glanced at Grant. "You got her back?"

"I've got his," I said. "There's no need to even send an escort to take me to the psych ward. I'll deliver myself there."

"And why should I trust you?" Noah asked.

"Because, after a week with me, you have to admit that If I wanted to leave, I would have by now."

25

G rant led me into the hospital and down the corridor, where armed guards were stationed at Gigi's door. "We already moved her."

"Gentry doesn't know that." I slowed my walk down the hallway and stopped in front of the picture of the man in question. Employee of the month. Had he really graduated from nursing school? Or maybe that was just another ploy for him to be as close to me as possible.

"He'd already been working as a nurse here before he got accepted into the program. It was in his file. He's only been assigned to this floor twice. We're lucky Gigi is still alive."

"Yes, we are."

Grant called off the guards on the room and sent them away. We stepped inside, and he handed me the hospital gown. I made quick work of changing and climbing into the bed. In one hand I had a gun; in the other, I had the syringe. It wasn't a matter of if Gentry would show up. Sam had already found him on the street cams around the hospital. He'd show and try to kill Gigi, and instead he'd get me.

It took two days of pretending to be a patient before I heard in my ear that Gentry was confident enough to make his move. Moonlight shone in through the curtains into the room. I tried my best not to stare over to where Grant was waiting in the bathroom. I closed my eyes with my finger on the trigger and strained to hear. I couldn't hear his footsteps on the floor as he approached the room. I couldn't hear anything, but I could feel. The anger intensified and grew like a virus worming through an apple. He was here; I sensed him.

The door creaked as it opened. I only had my gut and my intuition to help me. If I opened my eyes, he would know that it wasn't Gigi. He approached the bed and wrapped his fingers around my throat.

My eyes flew open, startling him, and I plunged the needle into his arm.

"How's that for being unpredictable?"

I lifted the gun and held it on Gentry as Sloan stepped in from behind the curtain separating the beds and Grant stepped out from the bathroom.

"Eh, Gentry should have predicted it," Sloan said. "After all, he all but drew you a map."

"Take me back to jail. I'll haunt you in your dreams like Carl does. We're connected, Lucy, until the day one of us dies, and I'll find a way out again," Gentry growled.

"Aw, that's sweet," I said, sitting up in the bed. "You think you're going to jail?" I chuckled. "I told you that you screwed up when you kidnapped the last girl. See Sloan here has a vested interest in what happens to you. Not only did you kill his niece, you took his assistant. So good luck with that."

Sloan twisted a silencer onto the end of his gun before he grabbed Gentry by his cuffed wrist. Two other men, with bulging muscles, appeared at the door with guns strapped in their arm holsters.

"Have a nice life, maybe what's left of it, anyway. I know I will." I waved as I slid off the bed.

26

I stared up at the psych ward building, inhaling a breath of fresh air. The greenery around the building seemed brighter today, or maybe it was the sun shining down instead of the clouds that normally blocked the light.

I knew I had to do it. I walked to the door, pulled it open, and headed straight for the receptionist desk. "Lucy Bray, I have a reservation."

It only took me two days to get back into the swing of things. I stood at the window with a grin from ear to ear as I watched Margo being placed in the psych ward van headed for a new detention center. For a split second, she stared up at me, and I lifted my pudding cup in cheers to say goodbye.

Margo tried to wrestle free, and I chuckled as she was strapped into a straitjacket. It was a sweet day for me. I turned toward Francine and headed her direction, placing an unopened pudding cup in front of her. "Two in one day, dear?"

"Margo won't be needing hers anymore."

"Neither will you." Noah's voice startled me from behind.

"Noah, what brings you by?"

He took his pen and raised the lanyard I'd hidden beneath my shirt. "Give it here."

"You know me so well," I teased and handed him the lanyard that gave me access to anywhere in the building. Noah took one look and tossed it to the orderly in the picture. "So, what gives? Did you miss me?"

Noah guided me out of the common area and toward my assigned room. "There were five bodies just dragged out of a lake."

In that moment I felt the familiar rumble of emotions flood through me like a dam that had broken free. It took my breath away. "Carl is awake."

"Yes, but he's under lock and key. This time it's personal," Noah said.

Not that it hadn't been last time. How much more personal could it get to track down someone obsessed with killing me? "What could be more personal than a man wanting to killing me?"

"Pack your bag and find out," Noah answered, turning into the room.

I grinned and grabbed the already packed suitcase sitting on the bed. "I bet you didn't know that I spent so much time emotionally embedded with you that I can feel the ghosts of your emotions pulling on me."

"Had I known, that you never would have made it out the front door." Noah said leading me back into the hallway and toward the exit.

I nudged his shoulder. "Don't worry; I'll keep your secret safe and sound."

"See that you do. I'd hate for you to disappear like Gentry." Noah raised a brow.

"Yeah, shame about that, isn't it? He must be more slippery than we thought." I then immediately changed the conversation. The last thing I needed was a pissed-off fed hounding me. "I'm guessing this next case has Carson Tines' name written all over it."

"I shouldn't be surprised you'd figure that out."

"Well, his emotions are all over the chart, but you should know...I have new demands."

"I'm not surprised."

I pulled the paper out of my pocket and handed it to him.

His jaw ticked as he read the paper. "You really were prepared."

"Just look at it this way. I'm not asking for my freedom. What trouble can I really get into if you authorize giving me a phone?" My laughter bounced off the white walls as I continued to the door.

Keep reading for a sneak peek at Killing Justice.

Killing Justice

27

"Which one of you dumped dad's body in the lake?" Carson asked, his somber tone void of emotion as he stared at his father's ghostly apparition.

Carson Tines and his two brothers stared slack-jawed, watching the horrific nightmare. Red and blue flashing lights bounced off the overhanging canopy of evergreen trees across the water. The gasoline smell from the Sheriff's Department boats and machinery drifted on the wind. Leashed barking dogs tugged their handlers toward the boat and bodies being lifted out of the water. The motion sent waves lapping against the shoreline.

For years people have gone missing from Carson's town. They weren't missing anymore.

"None of us put him in the lake," Michael answered. "We don't even know if any of those bodies are him."

His older brother's drunk optimism wasn't reassuring. As sure as Carson knew the sun would rise in the east, he knew the identity of at least one of the dead bodies the cops were fishing to retrieve.

Carson could feel it in his soul. They'd find five bodies beneath the murky water.

Bodies wrapped in blue tarps were being hauled out one by one. He and his brothers had known they'd eventually figure out their father's fate. They all knew their dad was near. How near, well, one of them must have known more than the other.

"I need a drink," his baby brother, Bishop, announced as he spun and stalked away.

They all did. A shot of whiskey, their father's favorite drink, to commemorate the day.

Michael and Bishop headed through the woods. Carson was slower to follow. Every time he returned home, he was ready to leave again. The painful memories consumed his thoughts, but being around his brothers made them worse.

"Janet is working behind the bar. Is that going to be an issue?" Michael asked.

Carson cursed. "My visit is temporary, but I'll be lucky if the lass doesn't spike my drink."

The bar was practically in their backyard, connected to their home by a well-worn path their father had carved out through the woods. As teens, Carson and his brothers had to retrieve their dad when he'd attempted to stumble home and inevitably passed out on the way. He excelled at drinking away his worries; that was the only life lesson he'd bestowed on his sons.

Carson stepped into the bar; his gaze went to the familiar clock on the wall in the shape of a cowgirl holding on to her hat. At the top of every hour, her leg would swing out, and the neon lights around her frame grew bright. Even that clock was worn with age. Scarred wooden stools lined the counter. One of the locals was hunched over at the end of the bar, nursing his frosty mug.

"Want to sit at the bar?" Bishop asked.

Carson shook his head. "No." He pointed to the table across the bar. "Over there, where we can talk."

Michael nudged him. "Grab the table, and I'll get the beers."

Carson crossed the room and spun the beat-up wooden chair around before straddling it. His gaze locked on Janet behind the bar, making sure she didn't poison his drink with arsenic.

She hadn't changed. Her red hair fell in waves down to her shoulders. Her bright green eyes had lost some of their light. Working in this place wore on a person. She was still beautiful, still sexy, and, judging by the tension in her jaw, still very stubborn.

As if she sensed Carson's thoughts, she lifted her gaze to meet his and narrowed those sexy, heated eyes. Carson tilted his head in acknowledgment, earning a deeper scowl.

"Do you think she's still pissed?" Bishop asked.

"Looks that way," Carson answered, taking a shot of whiskey and a bottle of beer from Michael before his brother scampered off to grab the rest of the drinks and join them.

Carson took a long swig of the cold beer before leaning into the table. This was a conversation they should have had years ago. Only then he hadn't been prepared to know the truth. Now it was a necessity.

"Listen, they'll think one of us killed him. They always look at family first. There's no denying we hated the bastard." Most of the time. "So, if one of you killed him, you need to tell me now so I can work out a plan to protect you."

"We don't even know if one of them was him," Bishop said, taking a sip of his beer.

Carson lifted a brow at Bishop's comment. His brothers might not know, but Carson did.

"Still, if it is him, we need a plan."

"Why are you so convinced they'll find Dad?" Michael asked. "Unless you know for a fact, he's in the lake."

Bishop leaned forward. His intense gaze landed on Carson like their father's had when dear old dad learned he'd been the one who flushed his alcohol down the toilet. "Did *you* kill him?"

The bar door flew open, and the sheriff walked in with two of his deputies. Behind him was Marine Recruiter, Master Sergeant Farley. He'd been the man who straightened Carson out all those years ago and sent him down a more rewarding path.

The sheriff scanned the room. His gaze held Carson's as he crossed the distance. "I heard you were back," Sheriff Anderson announced.

There was no love lost between the sheriff and Carson. Carson had been a known troublemaker growing up.

"Sheriff." Carson nodded. "I'm not here to start any trouble, just visiting my brothers."

"Give the kid a break, Sheriff. The Marines instilled a sense of duty in Carson a long time ago. He's no longer the punk you remember," Master Sergeant Farley announced. "Isn't that right, son?"

"Sir, yes sir." Carson rose from his seat and nodded.

Sheriff Anderson glanced over his shoulder at his daughter, Janet, before turning back around. "See that you keep your nose clean, Tines. I'd hate to throw you in jail."

The sheriff claimed that was where Carson would end up all along. He'd been wrong.

Carson retook his seat and grabbed his beer.

"I'm surprised you'd have time to worry about us seeing that your guys are dragging several bodies out of the lake," Bishop said, a little louder than necessary.

The patrons sitting nearby turned in their direction. One said, "Is that true, Sheriff?"

The diversion worked like a charm. Carson clinked his beer against Bishop's and grinned.

Sheriff Anderson gave Bishop a stinky side-eye before addressing the customers at the table. Carson's daddy and the sheriff had never seen eye to eye. Not since Carson's mom had died. Everyone in town blamed Carson's daddy for the deed. Hell, even his children had. Their dad had waited forty-eight hours before calling her in as missing. He'd been the last one with her before the cops had found her broken body on the side of the road the next day, and he hadn't had an alibi.

The questions paused when the door opened again, letting more sunlight into the dingy bar. The bar hadn't been this busy the last time Carson had visited.

As the door swung shut, a familiar face came into focus.

"Crap," Carson whispered beneath his breath. As if his day couldn't get any worse, it had doubled in a matter of seconds. Lucy investigating the dead bodies would bring results, and no matter if either brother was guilty, she'd figure it out. They were royally screwed. Carson rose from his seat. "Lucy, what are you doing here, and how did you escape?"

Lucy smiled in his direction. "You know, you didn't have to kill anyone to see me again. All you had to do was ask."

Bishop's and Michael's mouths parted as they stared at Lucy. Her shirt formed to her breasts, leaving little to the imagination. Her jeans, which were a little loose, showed swaths of her creamy skin. She was the girl next door and most men's wet dream.

Janet tilted her head and rested her hand on her hip.

"I never would have guessed you came from a small town, Carson. I thought you were conceived in a military experiment."

Michael laughed, and Carson knocked him in the gut before rubbing at the stress knot forming in his neck.

"Now, lass. How did you escape?" Carson asked as Lucy stepped farther into the bar with her handler, FBI Agent Noah Roth, and Sam, the IT guy, behind her.

"Did you say escape?" the sheriff asked.

"Escaping was the easy part," she said, glancing around the room. "We're connected, Carson, or have you forgotten?" She placed her hand over her heart and winked.

The entire bar was quiet as they watched Lucy walk

over to the table, pick up Carson's beer, and take a sip. "And from the looks of it, you could use our help."

Lucy stepped up to the sheriff and held out her hand. "Dr. Lucy Bray, Sheriff. The FBI and I look forward to working with you."

"Escaped from where?" he asked.

"Glendale psych ward." She patted his badge. "But don't worry. I'll grow on you."

"I doubt that," Sheriff Anderson answered.

"Can I just be the first to say that Carson didn't kill anyone. He's a big teddy bear."

"How did you even know we pulled dead bodies out of the lake? We're still collecting evidence." The sheriff's brows dipped.

"Yeah, well, then..." Lucy wrinkled her nose. "Carry on." Lucy waved her hand around the bar. "Which one of you sexy guys is going to buy me a glass of wine?"

"You're on the clock, Dr. Bray," Noah said, earning Lucy's frown.

Lucy loved her time away from the psych ward. She tended to push everyone's buttons and often. It was as if she could feel and taste the freedom that had been yanked away.

She sighed as she turned to meet his gaze. "I have no victim, no blood, nothing yet to play with, Noah."

"Agent Roth," he corrected.

"Noah, I think one glass of wine wouldn't hurt. Someone might even suggest it will help loosen me up for playtime."

"No one would say that, only you," Noah answered.

"Fine, I would say that," she said, turning back to the

guys in the bar. She surveyed each as if determining which one might be a threat and which might be the easiest guy to talk into buying her that drink.

"You haven't answered how the hell you know we pulled bodies out of the lake," the sheriff growled.

Lucy gestured to Noah. "That's above my pay grade. Oh, wait..." Her hand flew to her chest. "They aren't paying me a dime, so be a dear and talk to sparky over there."

"Why does she need blood and bodies?" Bishop whispered into Carson's ear.

Read book 2 in the Fractured Mind Series, KILLING JUSTICE. Get your copy at Amazon Today.

WANT TO READ WHAT JACK THOUGHT OF LUCY WHEN THEY FIRST MET? SIGN UP FOR MY NEWSLETTER TO GET THE BONUS CONENT.

(Once you sign up, my newsletter provider sends a confirmation email. Once confirmed, the bonus content is sent.)

There is a short delay for the confirmation email. Be sure to check your spam folder.

READ MORE BY KATE ALLENTON

Or maybe you like Psychics Cozy Reads? Check out Dead Wrong, Book I in the Cree Blue Psychic Eye Mystery Series.

Feel like adding a little Highlander Romance with your Cozy Psychic Mystery? Check out DEADLY INTENT, Book I in the Linked Inc. Series

Or maybe you'd like some straight up Romantic Suspense? Check out Deception, Book I in the Carrington-Hill Series.

ABOUT KATE ALLENTON

Kate has lived in Florida for most of her entire life. She enjoys a quiet life with her husband, Michael and two kids.

Kate has pulled all-nighters finishing her favorite books and also writing them. She says she'll sleep when she's dead or when her muse stops singing off key.

She loves creating worlds full of suspense, secrets, hunky men, kick ass heroines, steamy sex and oh yeah the love of a lifetime. Not to mention an occasional ghost and other supernatural talents thrown into the mix.

Sign up for her newsletters at www.kateallenton.com

She loves to hear from her readers by email at KateAllenton@hotmail.com, on Twitter@KateAllenton, and on Facebook at facebook.com/kateallenton.1

Visit her website at www.kateallenton.com

Made in the USA
Coppell, TX
06 June 2022

78534305R00100